SPOKEN

A NOVEL

MELANIE WEISS

Cover Design by Pixel Studios
Edited by Kathryn F. Galán, Wynnpix Productions
www.melanie-weiss.com

Published by Rosehip Publishing, Oak Park, Illinois

"Ode to the Midwest" from *Dear Darkness: Poems* by Kevin Young, copyright © 2008, by Kevin Young. Used by permission of Alfred A. Knopf, an imprint of the Knopf Doubleday Publishing Group, a division of Penguin Random House LLC. All rights reserved.
"Body of Work" by Jamael "Isaiah Mākar" Clark. Copyright © 2018 Jamael "Isaiah Mākar" Clark. *OPRF Spoken Word Chapbook, 2012-2013*. Compiled by David Gilmer for the poetry by Christian Thurman and Zoë Amundson. Copyright © Oak Park and River Forest High School, 2013.
"Taking Anxiety as a Lover" by Chelsea C. Bonner. *Poetry in Motion,* https://chelcbonnerpoetry.com. Copyright © Chelsea C. Bonner, 2018.
"Fried Shrimp" by Natalie Richardson. Copyright © Natalie Richardson, 2016.

PRINT ISBN 978-0-9886-0983-9

This book is dedicated to my family with love and to all those who believe in me. Back at ya.

A tough life needs a tough language—and that is what poetry is. That is what literature offers—a language powerful enough to say how it is. It isn't a hiding place. It is a finding place.

—Jeanette Winterson

SO, WHAT IS Spoken Word?

According to Urban Dictionary:

> Spoken Word is poetry intended for onstage performance, rather than exclusively designed for the page ... Due to its immediacy and direct rapport with its audience, this type of poetry often contains references to current events and issues relevant to a contemporary audience.
>
> At its best, spoken word is a powerful, high-energy form of expression that attracts artists and audiences of all ages from a wide range of disciplines and socio-cultural backgrounds.

— www.UrbanDictionary.com

PROLOGUE

A few months after we moved in with Mom's latest boyfriend, Kirk, Father's Day was coming up, and Mom sat me down for the "talk." I had asked her the dad question many times in my ten years. Basically, I knew his name, Marcel, and that he was French. Beyond that, Mom always gave me the same response: "One day, I'll tell you all about it."

Then she did.

The first thing I learned was that people actually live on cruise ships. The passengers come and go and come and go. But the crew and the staff and the performers stay put. I also learned that, when my mom was twenty, she was one of the dancers in the ship's musical theater shows who stayed. For months.

Mom said her favorite stop on the cruise was when they spent a day off the boat in Rome, Italy. So that's how I got my name, Roman.

Living on a big boat must get pretty boring. Mom and this musician Marcel, who was also working on the ship, spent a lot of time together. Long story short, after six months at sea, Mom came home to Chicago and Marcel went back to Arles. That's in France. They decided it would be too hard to stay in touch, I guess. This was before everyone had cell phones and the Internet even, which is crazy to think my mom is that old.

"I didn't know I was pregnant with you until weeks after I got back to Chicago. It was such a confusing time," Mom explained to me as we sat together on the bed in my new bedroom at Kirk's house. "Once you were born, I was scared to tell Marcel and find out he would want custody, too. I couldn't share you with someone who lives half a world away."

At first, that distance freaked me out, too. If Marcel learned about me being his son and claimed me as his own, who would I become? Where would I live? But as I grew older, I would look at a map and the ocean between us, and it seemed more and more like a stupid reason to keep me a secret.

I know one day I'll make the journey to meet him. Then, instead of a mystery, there will be my dad.

CHAPTER ONE

September 2013

I crash onto the brown leather sofa in the family room, even though I'm all sweaty from playing an hour of basketball with Sebastian. I jam a mound of Chunky Monkey into my mouth straight from the container. Those are two things I'm not supposed to do in my house.

Technically, this is Kirk's house, but my mom and I have lived here for four years, so, basically, it's my house, too. I'm watching, for the umpteenth time, *Catch Me if You Can,* which is one of Kirk's favorite movies. I figure that cancels out the other stuff I shouldn't be doing.

Rather than more hanging out, I know I need to deal with *The Iliad,* which Mrs. Lee assigned us last week in English. But if there ever was a quick fix for wanting to read, this 750-page epic Greek poem written a thousand years ago would do the trick. I mean, maybe in college you have to read a book like that. In ninth grade, it's just a sadistic teacher move. I'll look at the SparkNotes later on, which is probably what every single kid in the class will be doing.

I commit to the seventy-inch screen and burrow my whole body into the cushy sofa. I love this part, where a teenage con artist, played by Leo DiCaprio, starts to write his name on the chalkboard, introducing himself as the substitute teacher, even though he is really another student in the class.

Just as I'm comfortably comatose, I hear tires screech into the driveway. As I look out the window, Kirk jumps from his silver Mercedes sedan and rushes toward the house. Now *this* is weird, because Kirk is never home before dinner on a weekday, especially when he's directing a movie, like he is now, on the Universal backlot. I slide down lower on the couch, but he doesn't even glance my way. I watch as Kirk, his face flushed red, charges through the marble foyer and up the stairs toward the master bedroom suite. His hefty frame makes a loud thud on each step as he climbs.

I grab another full spoon of ice cream and return my attention to Leo, but then I hear the yelling.

"This is *shameful*, Steph!" Kirk screams at my mom.

The bedroom door slams shut. Now it's just muffled voices as they continue to argue. I drop the full spoon back into the sweating carton, not hungry anymore. This is ratcheted up way past their usual fighting.

I turn the volume up on the TV, hoping that will help me focus on what's in front of me instead of what's going on upstairs.

Then I see a few big drips of ice cream on the dark cushion between my legs.

"Shit!" I say to myself as I lean forward to mop up the mess with my T-shirt. My smearing has the wrong result. The white, sticky stain takes on a life of its own.

I don't need Kirk to see this and be pissed at me today, too. Mom's got him worked up enough about something.

I shift my thigh so it's covering the evidence. I'll deal with it later.

Turning my head to look up at the stairs, I wonder what annoying thing Mom did now. I'm caught off guard as I see her whip down the stairs, calling frantically from the hallway, "Roman, where are you?" Seeing me on the sofa, she rushes into the room. As she grabs my hand, my left thigh sharply separates from the sofa, and she pulls me up to my feet.

"We're leaving here. We have to go now."

Mom sniffles big. Her eyes are wet and red. She's wearing white shorts and a black tank top with the word *PINK* spelled out in pink rhinestones. Her dark hair is shoved into a messy ponytail. This is not how my mom would ever leave the house. Something bad happened.

"Pack some clothes," she says softly. "And your toothbrush."

Dazed, I stand my ground until she grabs my arm and marches me through the sparkling kitchen, with its white-marble countertops and two of everything—two fridges, two ovens, and even two dishwashers. Sunlight pours in through the many windows. I'm hurried past the kitchen island, with its four red-leather barstools. I've spent countless hours here, sitting on my butt and eating, doing homework, or just hanging out.

I'm not giving up all this awesomeness, am I?

Through the window, I see Kirk peel out of the driveway so fast, I think there is smoke coming off his tires.

I try to pull against my mother's grip on my arm, but she's an unstoppable force.

"Mom, what the hell did you do?"

"I don't want to talk about it now," she says as I trail down the hallway behind her until we are standing outside my bedroom door.

I'm so confused. Mom looks like hell. She's always been super-skinny. She says it's the dancer diet she never outgrew. But now she looks pale and shaky. On top of that, she's not even wearing makeup. I've never seen her walk out the front door without it.

"Mom, I'm not stupid. What's going on?" I ask. "Is this because of the McLaren? Damn it, Mom. You shouldn't have borrowed that car. It's Kirk's favorite."

A few weeks ago, Mom drove Kirk's orange McLaren coupe when her BMW was in the shop. It took her only minutes before she scratched the paint job pretty badly, when she backed into a bush along the edge of the garage. Oooh, was Kirk mad as hell. The car is in the shop now, being fixed, so maybe he got more bad news about the repair bill.

Mom shakes her head slowly, turns away, and trudges up the stairs. A few minutes later, she returns and hands me a magazine.

"We're going to Grandma and Grandpa's in Chicago, so pack up your stuff. I don't think we're coming back," she says as she retreats back to the stairs.

I look down at the wrinkled magazine Mom has handed me. *US Weekly*. Why would I want that? But then I see it. In the top right corner. A photo of *my mom* and some guy who is *not Kirk*. Kissing. The caption reads, "Joel Acosta's Affair with Movie Mogul's Girlfriend."

Good going, Mom. Great job. I drop the magazine on the floor and flop on my bed. Not only does my mom cheat on Kirk, who's only the unofficial king of Hollywood, but she does it with a married movie star. And she's so brainless, she gets caught by some trashy Hollywood paparazzi. Now everyone in L.A. knows about my mom screwing around. And anyone waiting in line at any supermarket in the whole damn country will get this shoved in their face, like it's entertainment.

But this isn't a game. This is my life.

CHAPTER TWO

Before this moment, every day with Mom and Kirk was so chill. Anytime I needed something, I could ask and I'd just get it. Whenever I wanted to go to a friend's house or the movies and Mom wasn't around, Kirk's assistant, Troy, if he wasn't busy, would take me. It was so awesome, and it was just my normal.

The next-door neighbors, Laurie and Paula, are songwriters who work with Selena Gomez and a bunch of other huge musicians. They have a barn and corral with three horses, and they sometimes asked me to ride the mare, Thunder, behind them while they took out Dolly and Madison on the horse paths that wind around the neighborhood.

I go to Calabasas High School with *two* kids whose dads played Major League Baseball, and one of my best friends has a mom who won an Oscar.

Ever since Mom's movie, *The Girl's Got Game,* came out this past summer, I gotta admit, things have not been the same around here.

After we moved in with Kirk, Mom went to tons of auditions and ended up in a bunch of commercials. Then, last year, she finally landed a pretty big movie role. Kirk swore he had nothing to do with her being cast. The buzz was that her screen tests were solid.

She was psyched about her feature film debut. That is, until she got some bad reviews for playing the tiger soccer mom who wants her daughter to be the star center forward. My mom would have to be a really good actress to pull off being a pushy, suburban soccer mom.

Mom hasn't been on an audition since. These days, she mostly sits by the pool with her friends, almost always her best friend Traci, or goes out to lunch or to shop or sometimes to yoga.

Now that I think about it, I kinda knew something had been going on with my mom and Joel. In the spring, Kirk was filming a movie in Toronto. During school vacation, my mom took me to Disneyland. We both had VIP passes, so we could walk up to the red velvet ropes and be the next ones on any ride.

She took so many pictures—I think she had me pose for one on every ride. That night, on the car ride home, I picked up her phone, looking for a new Facebook profile picture. I was zipping through her photos when I saw her standing next to this guy with his arm around her waist on some beach. She also had a selfie of the two of them sitting outside, eating frozen yogurt at Menchies, which is where she always takes me, because I like pouring different yogurt flavors in the dish and then flooding the bowl with rainbow sprinkles.

"Hey, Mom, who's this?" I asked her, holding up the Menchies photo.

She looked at it and then quickly whipped her eyes back onto the road. "Oh," she stammered. "That's my friend, Joel." She started gripping the steering wheel really tight. "You know, he was in that movie I filmed in New Orleans? He was the soccer coach?"

But she said it like a question, and her voice went all high and strange-sounding. Then she changed the subject and asked me what my favorite ride of the day had been.

That was the thing, how her voice went all weird and how quickly she changed the subject, that made something in my brain go "ding, ding, ding..." It just didn't feel right...

As I think about all this, I'm lying on my bed, looking up at the ceiling.

"Roman, five minutes," Mom says, standing outside my door. She heads to my closet, pulls out a Nike gym bag, and tosses it next to me on the bed with a weak smile. Then she walks out.

I force myself to stand up. How do I pack my world into this dinky bag? I carry it to the bathroom and flip on the light switch. The bright lights bounce off the glass-enclosed shower and reflect onto the huge mirror above the sink.

I open a drawer and take out my toothbrush and toothpaste and throw them in the bag. Then I toss in some deodorant, because I don't want to stink when I wake up tomorrow who-knows-where.

Back in my bedroom, I pull open my dresser drawers and mechanically toss clothes inside until the bag is full. Sinking my toes into the white, plush carpet settles me down a bit.

Our housekeeper, Cora, walks in with a brown paper bag. "I made you your favorite chicken burrito, Mr. Roman." She hands me the bulging bag and then gives me a hug, her plump arms squeezing me tight. We look into each other's eyes, knowing these will likely be our last minutes together, and exchange sad smiles.

"This is messy, yes?" she says.

"Looks that way," I answer. "Thanks for this." I hold up the paper bag. "For everything, too."

If Cora had her way, she would have fed me until I eventually exploded. Cora loves to make Mexican food with cheese and sour cream and guacamole. She makes killer tortillas and chips, and my mom has always complained about how she cooks with lard. All I know is it all tasted really amazing. And I realize I'll never get to taste any of it again.

"I talked to Troy," adds Cora. "He isn't working today. He wants me to tell you to think of him as a friend. To keep in touch."

Standing next to Cora, I suddenly have this huge craving to crawl into bed and stay there, like I would when I was sick. Cora made it so that being sick didn't suck. She would cook me chicken soup with tons of vegetables, and I'd eat all of it because I knew, later, she'd bring one of her chocolate banana milkshakes through my door. A few times when I was sick and Cora wasn't working, Mom would make me a milkshake, too, but she'd sneak some healthy shit into it like avocado, and that just ruined it.

"It's one thing to share Miss Stephanie's good looks," she says, stroking my dark hair once. "Just watch out you don't have her crazy heart, too."

Cora gives me a second squeeze, grabs a tissue from her pocket, and walks out the door, sniffling.

I get that Cora is worried about me, but "don't be nuts like your mom" is not the kind of advice I need right now.

I try to shake off her words and focus on the incredible smells wafting from her warm paper bag. I know it's time to leave, but I'm frozen in place.

I fell in deep right away and didn't let myself even think it might just be too good to last. I've lived this before, Mom's upending my world for a guy. Now I'm being reminded I don't belong here and I don't belong to Kirk.

Before Mom started dating Kirk, she was with this guy, Pasquale, for a year or so. He lived with us on the weekends and spent more time in front of our bathroom mirror than both Mom and me combined. He was a model and had been on a bunch of commercials for products like Coors, McDonald's, and Tostitos. Even Mom got sick of how obsessed Pasquale was with Pasquale. But she didn't kick him to the curb until she met Kirk.

At first, I was really happy about Kirk for that reason alone. But then, pretty soon after he started dating Mom, Kirk took us both to a Lakers game on the day they won their division. We sat in these amazing seats four rows from center court, and Kirk bought me a Ron Artest jersey. (This was way before he changed his name to Metta World Peace.) Kirk asked me questions about school and what I liked to do and seemed interested in my life.

I sit on the end of my bed and look around one last time. The shiny, white-lacquer furniture in my bedroom was here when we moved in and always felt too girly for me. One of the first things Mom and I did after we walked into this *heaven on Earth* with our suitcases more than four years ago was buy me a blue-plaid bedspread and throw my Lakers pennant and a Porsche poster up on the wall.

The room was big enough that, in the corner between the door to my room and my bathroom door, we could fit a table and two swivelly chairs just for gaming. Sebastian and I spent hours in those chairs, playing *FIFA, Motorsport,* or quick scoping one-on-one death matches. Just last week, we were ROFL after we got beat and out-cursed in a death match against two six-year-olds in Missouri.

I stand and take a step forward, so my face is framed in the huge gilded mirror above the dresser. People are always telling me, "You look *just* like your mother" and "Your mom is so beautiful—you're so lucky you take after her." But to be honest, I really wish I could look in a mirror and see something that doesn't remind me of my mom.

I mean we both have the same glossy, black hair and green eyes shaded by eyelashes that, as Mom's agent says, "just won't quit." But I want to look at my reflection and see something of my dad there; something *we* share. I'm sure I have some feature or trait of his. Maybe we have the same nose? The same jaw? The same hairy arms?

If he were around, maybe people would be saying, "You have your dad's smile..." or "I can tell you're going to be tall like your dad...."

What I *do* know is, even though I may look like I got a lot of my mom's DNA, that is only half of who I am.

CHAPTER THREE

I snap back into reality and pick up my laptop. Eyeing my two TV monitors and external speakers, which give me an edge since they tell me exactly where every sound is coming from, I know there's no way my tricked-up gaming setup can come with. It's so unfair that this huge piece of my world gets to stay while I have to leave.

I plod out to the driveway. Mom's BMW convertible is completely stuffed. I make some room to stash my laptop, gym bag, and the paper lunch bag from Cora alongside the suitcases and purses and coats Mom's thrown on top. Mom has changed into yoga pants and brushed her hair out, but she still has the PINK tank top on. She stands in front of the car, looking out at the L.A. skyline we can see clearly from the front of Kirk's house, since it's situated up in the Hills.

I walk over to the passenger door, but it all feels wrong. I have to let Mom know what a mistake she's making.

"Why can't we just go to Traci's and stay there? I mean, really, Mom. I just started high school last month," I plead. "Why do we have to go to Chicago?" It's hard for me to ask her this. I know she's hurting, but I also know she's about to blow up my life.

She looks at me and says flatly and so softly I can barely hear her, "Roman, I'm really sorry to do this. I hate it. But how can I stay in L.A. now, with this gossip all over the place? I have to get far away from here. You can understand that."

She cautiously walks over and hugs me real tight. I stand straight as a rod and don't hug her back. Mom steps away, and I notice her mascara is smudged from crying. She smells like those cinnamon bun stores at the airport. I guess I shouldn't be surprised she made time during our morning of complete chaos to put on makeup and douse herself with her favorite sickeningly sweet perfume.

"I need all this to die down a bit." She looks over at the house behind us, avoiding my gaze. "I have to disappear from L.A. for a while—I just do!"

The basketball Sebastian and I were just using sits a few feet from the front door. I go to pick it up.

"Leave it," Mom says sharply. Then she softens her tone and adds, "We can get you one, but that's Kirk's. For his court."

And just like that, it's his court and his basketball, when I'm the one who has used it almost every day. Playing pickup with Alex and Sebastian for hours. When after any of us hit a three-pointer, we'd wait a beat for Alex to yell, "Kobe!" and then blast his hands up to the sky.

I want to argue but don't. There's a lot I want to say but know it won't make any difference. It'll only make her madder and me sadder. Or maybe me madder and her sadder. Who knows? It's all twisted anyway.

Like the fact that my fifteenth birthday is coming up in less than two weeks. To celebrate, Mom and Kirk were going to take me to a Dodgers game. It's my birthday tradition. But this was going to be even more amazing, because Kirk got seats right behind the Dodger dugout, and Sebastian was going to come with us. We would have been so close to all the players. Kirk promised me we would get there early enough to get a bunch of players' autographs.

Just today at lunch, I was telling Alexandra and Carly about how I'd be sitting right up in the action, and Alexandra was way impressed. It takes a lot to have a hot girl like that think anything is a big deal. I mean I went to her eighth-grade graduation party and her house seriously has a lake and an indoor bowling alley. Her parents own some big vitamin company, and I heard her dad has a golf room with a bunch of putting greens and video screens. After being at her party (with some big name EDM DJ, a tricked-out taco bar, a guy in a hut making smoothies, and an ice cream truck), I would be surprised if he didn't.

Alexandra was totally excited I was going to be inches away from the players. She grabbed my phone right out of my hand to punch in her number, so I could text her pictures from the field. Well, that's obviously not gonna happen. Me and Alexandra are not going to happen, either.

I take in the BMW, jam-packed to the roof with what we can fit from our lives here. This is what's happening. I don't know when I will see all my friends next. On top of that, not only do we not have the big Hollywood house anymore, but we don't have a house at all. Mom really fucked up everything.

She opens the car door. With a fake grin plastered on her face, she motions for me to get in and lowers herself into the driver's seat.

"When am I going to see Kirk again?" I ask as I open my car door. I stand next to the front passenger seat, knowing my next move will take me away from here. "When are we coming back?"

"Roman, please get in the car. We can stop at In-N-Out before we get on the highway."

Like a stupid burger's going to make any of this less awful.

She leans toward me and says in her most serious tone, "We can't be here when Kirk gets home. I promised him that."

"Did he even say anything about me?" I slump into the passenger seat, scraping at my wet cheeks with the back of my hand.

"Yes, of course. He wants to talk with you once we get settled. He's just upset right now. We have to give him some space."

"What did Grandma say about you cheating on Kirk?"

She doesn't say anything more until we're clear of the palms lining Kirk's driveway.

"Honey, I screwed up. I know that. I need my mom and dad like I have never needed them before." She touches my knee. "And I need you, too."

We stop at the end of the drive, waiting for a car to pass by. I finally look over at her.

Mom meets my gaze, both of us with watery eyes, and I whip my head away to stare out my car window. She pulls out a few tissues from a pack in her purse and puts one in my lap. I brush it onto the floor mat. Bring on the blurry vision. It shields me from watching my whole world disappear.

She turns up the air conditioning and lets the cool air blast in our faces for a few minutes while we stare out at the wonderland of estates before us. Through teary eyes, I take a mental picture, wanting to soak in this great big reality I thought would never end. Then we pull onto the road, and she lets out a big sigh.

On the way out of the North Gate, we pass rapper Drake's house, aka YOLO Estate. He had that printed on a plaque and nailed to the fence in front of his house, but after it got stolen three times, he never replaced it. My mood lifts for a minute when I think about how funny it was when Amber, the daughter of Mom's friend Sherry, stole the sign once with a group of friends. When she proudly brought it home, Sherry made her return it with a note of apology.

Now I get to sit in the car for more than twenty-four hours, because the only place my mom says she can feel safe is with her parents, and they live in Boringville, USA. I know because I lived there when I was real little, and there is no basketball court and definitely no pool. Honestly, the most thrilling thing Grandpa and I did when we visited last year was play Bananagrams.

CHAPTER FOUR

We've barely merged into the carpool lane of Highway 405 before my phone starts blowing up.

"Dammit, Mom," I say. "Everyone is texting me." I look down at my constantly buzzing phone. Friends and friends of friends are wanting to know, "How are you?" and "What are you doing?" and "Can I come over and talk?"

I bury my phone underneath a pile of luggage in the backseat.

The only person I really feel like texting is Kirk. I mean I want to know: Are we okay?

Kirk is the closest thing to a father I've ever had, and you can't get much cooler than Kirk. Yeah, he has a big belly and no hair and all, so I know my mom couldn't be attracted to all that. But he is *the man* in Hollywood, and Mom loved that so much. I once heard her tell Grandma how magical it is to live in his world. I know there were times after we first moved in when Mom told him she wanted to get married, but Kirk is not shy about telling anyone who wants to listen that he's gotten burned a few times in the marriage department and has "wised up from that gig."

Kirk has four other kids, but they are *old*, like my mom. He would take me to work with him sometimes to the movie sets, and there would be Jennifer Lawrence or Chris Pine. Once, I even saw Johnny Depp. I would hang out and watch them set up a scene, and then they would start the scene and stop it and start it again, over and over. It did get boring kind of quick. But there were always tables filled with the best catered food, and lots of it, so I could sit there and stuff my face.

Sometimes, the movies Kirk made had other kids in them who I could hang out with on the lot. Once in a while, I would help some of the minor actors practice their lines, and I thought maybe I wanted to be an actor, too. I told Kirk, and he gave me a small role as the kid next door in his next movie. Maybe I wasn't too good, though, because after I said my two lines over and over again like fifteen times, they said "great" and patted me on the back.

Then, when I saw the movie a year later in Kirk's private screening room, there was my scene, but instead, some blonde, freckly girl was saying those same lines. Nobody ever told me why, and I was like thirteen, so I didn't know if I should ask about it, and I just stayed quiet. But I really would like to know if I was *that* bad an actor or did they just decide a girl would be better in that scene?

That's how Kirk met my mom. She had a small part in one of his movies. The main character hits on her in a bar, and she has a one-night stand thing with him. I was in fourth grade then, but I never saw the movie because it was rated R. Also, my friend Jeffrey told me when the movie first came out that he heard his parents talking about how my mom was naked in the bed. That's something I don't ever need to see.

"Mom, this music sucks," I say, punching button after button on the car radio as we whiz past signs pointing to Las Vegas. I've eaten my take-out burgers and Cora's burrito, taken a nap, and now I am insanely bored. "Can we play my music?"

"Sure," she says. "Just none of that rap stuff you listen to. It gives me a headache."

"But Mom, you like some of it. Remember I made you that playlist with Drake, Eminem, and Kendrick Lamar?"

She always lumps all rap music together. It's so old lady of her.

I pull my phone out from where I stuck it in the backseat. "Twenty-seven messages! A personal record," I say.

Mom grabs her iPhone from the center console and hands it to me. "Okay, big shot, how many messages do I have?"

"Holy crap! Mom… You have fifty-two."

She laughs. "Roman," she says and then pauses. "I owe you an explanation for all this. I know that. The minute I met Joel, we just hit it off. I didn't want that to end after the film wrapped and thought we could hang out and be friends."

As she's talking, the towering piles in the backseat shift forward, and I turn around to push the cascading jackets and bags away from my head. I stare out the window for a few miles of billboards advertising pit stops like McDonald's and Super 8 Hotels, the meaning buried in her last sentence hanging in the air.

Mom breaks the quiet. "Traci told me that, unconsciously, I meant to get caught. And who knows? Maybe I did. I loved the way Kirk took care of me, of us, especially in the beginning. But it just got too ordinary. We weren't meant to be together for this long."

"It's like Grandpa always says, go big or go home," I say as I turn my head in her direction. "And it is kinda sad, Mom, because now you are going home."

She misreads my steely gaze for sympathy and beams at me warmly. I am not ready to forgive her. I am still pissed as hell. We're driving away from the life I had and the life I loved. What we are driving toward I have no idea.

I flip up the volume knob and hit a button, so the car's Bluetooth syncs to my iPhone. "Juice" by Chance the Rapper blares throughout the car.

I don't change it.

CHAPTER FIVE

Mom's definitely stopped beaming at me. Instead, she's gritting her teeth while Chance blasts out his lyrics.

When "Lose Yourself" from Eminem starts up next, she shakes her head no and then continues shooting down every rap song in my playlist.

Except for "Thrift Shop" by Macklemore, Mom doesn't even give my music a chance, dissing each song within the first ten seconds.

Finally, I get smart and pull a tangled pair of white earbuds from the car's glove box so I can listen to my music in peace.

For a few days, we drive miles out of our way to find the nicest hotels, checking into rooms that have two queen beds with white, fluffy comforters and four pillows on each bed. "No two-star hotels for us," Mom would say. Each night, Mom preorders us a room service breakfast that's delivered with a wake-up call at exactly 9 a.m.

On day three, when we're somewhere outside Des Moines, Iowa, we drive up to the ATM, and Mom whips out her bank card. She looks at the receipt before crumpling it up and throwing it on the floor of the car. That night, we stay at a Holiday Inn Express right off the highway, where the rumbling of cars and trucks keep me up half the night. I wake up tired but figure I'll have five hours in the car to catch up on my sleep before we get to Grandma and Grandpa's.

"Hey, Mom, where's the sun?" I ask, waking up to gray skies as we get close to Oak Park, the suburb outside Chicago where she grew up. In Los Angeles, the whole world sparkled; the water, the beach, and even the streets were bright and gleaming. But as we continue to head east, everything out my window just looks dull and gloomy.

"When we get to Grandma and Grandpa's, check out the stars at night," Mom says. "When I was on the cruise ship, I spent so many nights just staring up at the stars. There would be hundreds of them twinkling over our heads. I've missed that, living in L.A.! Too much light pollution."

I turn to fish around in my duffel bag, find the one sweatshirt I brought, and pull it over my T-shirt. "The nights may have more stars out here, but do the days have to be so cold?" I complain.

"Oh, we just have L.A. blood. That's what happens when you live in a place where it's summer all year round. You'll get used to this. I promise."

That's one promise I'd be happy for her not to keep. No way do I want to get used to being cold or, even worse, get used to living anywhere but L.A.

Later that afternoon, we pull into Grandma and Grandpa's driveway. It leads to the gingerbread-color, two-story, square, brick home they have lived in for longer than my mom has been alive. The car doors open in sync as we both jump out of our seats. We're tired after hours and hours of being cooped up with each other and our worries.

Grandma Brenda greets us from the front porch. She wears a short, black-quilted jacket with red buttons fastened up to her neck, so I can tell she has been outside, waiting for us. She walks up to Mom, and they stand together in a hug for a really long time. I'm next but try to scoot out of Grandma's arms pretty quickly.

But there's no escaping. She pulls me back and gently holds my elbows as she looks me in the eyes. "Roman," she says.

"Grandma," I answer, returning her gaze. I always feel comforted by her loving smile, welcoming eyes, and soft touch. Still, I pull away after a bit and avert my eyes to take in the action in front of the house.

Grandma has hung two bird feeders, and they swing on low branches of the tree in the middle of her front lawn. I get a kick out of watching the little brown birds hop around in the birdseed that has fallen to the ground.

As we bring our bags into the house, my mind plays games with me right away. I always feel like I'm in a funhouse when I visit. The walls are whiter, the rooms smaller, and the ceilings lower than at Kirk's, so at first everything feels kinda mini. The bleached-wood furniture, what Grandma calls "modern," feels minimal and cold compared to the overstuffed, oversized furniture and abundance of shiny surfaces I'm used to, not just at Kirk's but at all my friends' uber-decorated L.A. houses.

I know the drill, so I trudge up the sand-colored carpeted stairs to the guest bedroom, with Grandma following behind me. It used to be Mom's older brother Jason's room, but he now lives in Milwaukee.

Grandma has turned it into her sewing and meditation room. She ruffles my hair as she sits down next to me on the gray sofa bed. She's done that since I was little, and now I kinda hate it, because she messes it up. She wraps her arm around me to give me a hug, and I lean slightly into her shoulder. Her brown hair pokes me uncomfortably in the face, but I don't pull away.

"Grandpa's working at the college, but he'll be home soon," she says. "He can't wait to see you. We're really glad you're both here. This is a tough time for your mom. And I know it can't be easy for you, either."

She's got that right.

"Honey, this is all going to be okay."

I'm not buying it. You can't just say, "Everything's okay," and then magically it is.

"No, Grandma, it won't be." I pull away, unlatching from her hold. "My life has basically ended, thanks to Mom."

We sit there in silence as I glare into space.

"Roman Santi!" Grandma barks. "You're going to have to be patient with your mom while she sorts this mess out."

Then she hands me the dog's leash and a plastic baggie from her other hand. "Why don't you go walk Ozzie? The fresh air will do you both good."

"Fine," I answer sharply, standing up. I'm happy for the excuse to get away from this pity party Grandma is having for Mom.

On my walk around the block with big, old, brown Ozzie sniffing every blade of grass like the old mutt he is, I pass other people walking their dogs and the slightly varied versions of my grandparents' brick house that line both sides of the streets, all set among tall, leafy parkway trees and lawns, some well-kept and others weedy and wild. In every possible way, I am light-years from the perfectly landscaped estates in Calabasas, where ginormous homes are often hidden beyond gates and up snaking driveways.

Not only do I walk Ozzie, but he goes and takes a shit. Then I have to clean it up. Picking up his gross poop is something I'm going to have to get used to doing.

And that isn't my only chore. I have to make my bed here. I would wake up in my house in L.A. and go have breakfast or something and come back to my room later, where my bed would be like I'd never slept in it, with the sheets all tight and tucked in smooth with no wrinkles. It was fun to think it just was the magic bed that got made; that was where my head went with that. Now I know beds don't get magically made, because whenever I visit Oak Park, my bed is never tight and cozy to climb into at night. I just throw the comforter over and leave the sheets all bunched up underneath.

Since Mom needs "time to think" and to "figure things out," I'm trading in my plush L.A. private spaces for a musty guest room with an exercise bike in one corner and a sewing machine in the other, while I sleep on the lumpy, pullout sofa in the middle.

After walking Ozzie, I head back upstairs to check my phone. Since her bedroom is right next to mine, I can hear Mom talking to someone, probably Traci. "It's such a betrayal!" she says, her voice making no effort to be quiet on the other side of the paper-thin wall.

Needing to tune out more Mom drama, I pick up my toothbrush, half-full tube of Crest toothpaste, and "Ultimate Sport" Speed Stick, and head into the bathroom. Mom's shitload of lotions and makeup already clutter the white countertop around the bathroom sink. I manage to eke out a few inches of space in the one corner she didn't invade.

Looks like I'm supposed to go from living like a rock star to living in this old, vanilla house with my grandparents and act like everything is okay.

CHAPTER SIX

I'm hiding out in the guest room, playing *Angry Birds* on my phone, when Mom walks into the bedroom holding a set of blue sheets. I help her flip open the sofa bed, and she throws me one side of the fitted sheet to pull over the thin mattress. Together, we work in silence to make up the bed. I can tell she's worn out and we are both past the point of conversation.

Just as we are finishing up, Grandpa Marty walks in to lighten the mood. He goes to Mom first, and they hug before he comes over and grabs me in his arms, too. Grandpa is a tall, dark, and skinny Italian guy who doesn't do anything subtly. He eats with gusto, commands his students to attention with a look, and, since he was a runner in high school, still enters 5K races whenever he can, hoping to get a PR (that's a personal record).

He also loves anything science fiction, which I guess makes sense, since he is a science teacher. He drags me to every *Star Trek/Star Wars/Lord of the Rings* movie, and they are like three hours long (or, if they aren't, they feel like they are). I don't really like that fantasy stuff, but I fake it because I love my grandpa.

"How's my grandson doing?" he asks as Mom quietly slips out of the room after announcing she's going to help with dinner.

"Oh, I'm great, Grandpa," I joke to him. One thing about my grandpa is I can always talk to him straight.

"I know, kid. This totally bites. Your mom did a job on things, didn't she?"

I laugh. But then I get serious. I need Grandpa to be the voice of reason and talk to Mom.

"Grandpa, I really don't know why we had to come all this way. I get that Mom is embarrassed, but she just, like, ran away. She didn't even think about me. She didn't care I had to leave my friends and my school. I like it there, you know. A lot."

Grandpa sits at the end of my bed, and I slide down next to him, awaiting his support.

"I'm with your mom here, Roman. I realize you don't see it now, but your mom's world is rocked, you know?"

I nod. I can tell Grandpa is trying to talk "my language," even though he's missing by a mile.

"But Grandpa, I have a life, too. And it's in L.A."

"Yes, I know you do. But Mom needs to build her own career. Living with Kirk wasn't really the best your mom can do for herself. Or for you," he adds.

"But it *was* the best. It was perfect." I try but can't stop the flood of tears that start to roll down my face.

"Oh, there's no tissues in here. Let me get us some."

"No, forget it. I'm okay. Thanks, Grandpa." I wipe away the drippy streaks with the sleeve of my sweatshirt and will myself to stop the crying.

"Okay, well, dinner's in ten minutes." He stands up. "You'll get through this, Roman," he says." We'll get through this together."

I look down at the ground and shake my head, wanting him to leave so I can be alone. Everyone is on Mom's side. I thought Grandpa would be my champion. I thought he would help me get back to L.A.

In fact, I was banking on it.

CHAPTER SEVEN

Mom and I sit with my grandparents around the rectangular wooden table in the center of the white-tiled kitchen floor. We pass around serving bowls of baked chicken, steamed broccoli, and macaroni and cheese.

It's a pretty quiet meal, with some talk about the places we stopped during our three days of driving from L.A. Then Mom starts to rant.

"I'm pretty sure it was Troy who ratted me out to the magazine."

"Mom, you don't know that," I say, quickly coming to his defense. Troy never got along with Mom. That was obvious in the way he always snubbed her. Still, she shouldn't blame him for her bad luck.

"Yeah, I agree with Roman," Grandpa says. "Don't look for someone to pin this on."

"Well, it's more than that," Mom says. "That picture is from the day I scratched the McLaren. I was shaken up and not really thinking when I asked Joel to pick me up at the house. We drove out to the beach so I could clear my head. Troy was around, so I told him that Joel and I had some movie business in Century City. I think he tipped off the paparazzi and had me followed."

"Well, you'll never know for sure, Mom, will you?" I try to put this topic to rest. I like Troy.

"Actually, Roman. I feel like I do know." She looks at me with her fork suspended in midair. "For sure." She stabs at a piece of broccoli to cement her point.

Oh. I guess *now* this conversation is over. "What other fun things can we talk about?" I want to add, but it's a pretty safe bet nobody else at this table is in the mood for my jokes tonight.

CHAPTER EIGHT

I wake up around noon surrounded by worn carpeting and faded photographs hanging on the wall. I really need a dose of my L.A. life right now, so I pull out my phone and text Kirk.

> *Hey, can you send me my PlayStation? I'm at my grandparents.*

>> *Hi Champ. Sure thing. Troy will send it tomorrow. Hope you are doing OK out there.*

> *Thanks :)*

Three days later, my PlayStation shows up along with a new, huge, forty-inch TV. I can tell Grandma, Grandpa, and Mom are not happy about putting the mega-TV in Grandma's "meditation room," but they also know it's all I have right now to be happy about, so they zip their lips. Grandpa and Mom help me set it up atop the dresser. The TV stand takes up the whole top of the dresser and spills over on both sides. It's awesome!

Kirk also sends me a suitcase. Inside is a #16 Lakers jersey from my favorite player, Pau Gasol, folded on top of a bunch of clothes from my room back at home. (Well, in L.A., which was home.) On the bottom of the suitcase, I find a note scribbled in black pen.

> *Have a great birthday. I do miss you, kid!*

In the suitcase is the framed photograph I had on my dresser of me and some of my friends—Sebastian, Alex, Noah, and Lucas—all with shit-eating grins on our faces.

The picture was taken on my eleventh birthday, which was also the first one I spent living with Kirk. I had, like, ten friends over, and we all went swimming in the infinity pool, or at least that's what Mom always calls it. Then we watched *The Avengers* in Kirk's screening room and threw popcorn and Skittles all over the place.

I remember Kirk came in the room, carefully stepping around the food scattered all over the floor, and I was scared he was going to be mad that we'd messed up his space. Instead, he took out his iPhone and told us to pose while he snapped our picture.

I search what I hope is my temporary bedroom, needing a place of honor for the photograph. Grandma's Buddha statue sits on top of the built-in bookshelf. I push it back and place the framed photo prominently in sight.

Then I shoot Kirk a text.

The TV is so huge! It's great. Thanks.

After a minute or so, I stop staring down at my phone, waiting for his response. I guess Kirk's busy.

CHAPTER NINE

L iving in Oak Park is nothing new for me. After my mom found out she was pregnant, she moved in with Grandma Brenda and Grandpa Marty. Grandma has always said Mom is "a really talented dancer" and "too pretty for her own good." Grandma told me, if mom wasn't so pretty, maybe she would have gone to college after high school graduation and not gotten bit by the acting bug so hard.

When my mom was eighteen, she was in a summer production of *A Chorus Line* at an outdoor theater in St Louis. Then she caught the eye of some talent scout, who got her a part in a show in Las Vegas that got canceled nine months after she moved out there. A few of the backup dancers, including her new friend Traci, were hired to perform on a cruise ship, and my mom decided to go with them. Once I came into the picture, Mom realized she needed to move back home to make a new plan.

Three months after I was born, Mom did become a college student at Concordia University in nearby River Forest. She got a degree in sociology and acted in all the college productions. We would go watch her in her plays at Lund Auditorium, sitting in the center of one of the first few rows. Grandma always made me sit through Mom's plays from start to final bows at the end, even though I had no clue what was going on up there. I was usually bored out of my skull, with nothing to do but pick from a plastic dish of Cheerios or Goldfish crackers on my lap.

Grandma used to be a yoga teacher. After Mom graduated from high school, she stopped doing that and began volunteering a lot at the local food pantry, so she watched after me more than Mom did.

I spent a lot of time with my grandparents when Mom was in school and acting in her plays. It was my grandpa who taught me how to ride a bike, how to throw a baseball, and who took me to my first 3D movie. He was a high school chemistry teacher, but he retired a few years ago and now teaches at a community college. Even back then, he always had so much free time in the summer to take me to the zoo and parks. We also went to the food pantry a lot with Grandma B, sorting food into the right bins.

By the time I was five, it was off to Hollywood. Mom was sure she would make it big in no time.

Mom did get lucky, I guess, as she was cast in a commercial pretty quickly, and even though it was for girl stuff I won't mention, it was on TV a lot. She got something called residuals that allowed her to rent a decent apartment in Glendale, and she bought a yellow convertible called a Spider, but I think it was spelled like *Spyder*. All the closets in our apartment (even mine) were filled with her clothes, most of which were small and sparkly. (I did get a dresser, though.)

That's an annoying thing about my mom. She's all about the bling. That's what Grandma always calls it. "Bling." Grandma does not hide the fact that it drives her crazy, too.

When we started living in the shiniest place on Earth, Mom was so excited to have found her peeps. Then we moved, starry-eyed, into Kirk's killer crib in Hidden Hills. I remember a few years ago, when Traci came to Kirk's for Thanksgiving dinner. By then, Traci was a choreographer for music videos, which I've told Mom a million times is a much cooler job than being an actress.

Traci walked in, carrying a huge platter covered with aluminum foil, took one look at Mom, and said, "Steph, it's a Puritan holiday… Why do you always dress like we're going to a beach party?"

I laughed, because I actually knew who the Puritans were, having learned about that in American history. I pictured the men in their black-buckle belts and women in their white smocks and then looked at Mom, in her ridiculously short, gray tank dress banded with rows of horizontal gray sparkles. Traci smiled at me like we had a private joke together. But Mom just stuck her tongue out at her, which is what she does when she doesn't have a snappy comeback because she knows you are right.

So now, it's weird to see my mom being sparkle-less. It's been more than a week since we got to Oak Park. Mom's been moping around the house in black yoga pants and flowy tops she borrows from Grandma. She's been sleeping later than I do and has gone days without makeup. I've just stayed out of her way.

This morning, Mom walks into my room, as I'm slowly waking up and checking Instagram, and sits on the edge of my bed.

"Roman, I've been wanting to tell you this for a few days, but I know it's a sore subject. It's over with Joel. We realize what a mess we've made of everything."

"What about Kirk? Have you talked to him?" I ask, sitting up quickly and putting away my phone. I don't care anything about Joel. But Kirk was like my dad, and Mom hurt him bad.

"Yes. We've talked. He's still angry with me. It was really ugly how it all went down. He's also upset I uprooted you, but he realizes I need my parents' support for all this. He wants me to, well, as he said, get it together. And I want that, too. That's why we're here. So, I can do that."

As we're talking, Grandpa Marty walks by my room and sticks his head in to say good morning, waving the arts section of the *Chicago Tribune* in my direction.

"Be right down, Grandpa," I answer. Mornings are when we solve the newspaper crossword and Jumble together. Since I'm not in school, Grandpa says I need to keep my brain sharp. With him on my case, I can barely find time to mess around on my laptop.

Tomorrow, Mom wants to register me in high school here—her and Jason's old high school. I don't know if this is for a week, a month—maybe longer?

My old life is slipping away. How I get back to it is looking pretty fuzzy right now.

CHAPTER TEN

"Fifteen, huh? How did this happen?" Mom stands outside my partially open bedroom door.

I am lying on the open sofa bed in a Toronto T-shirt (Kirk brought it back after he finished filming there) and shorts, watching a rerun of *How I Met your Mother*.

"Ha-ha, Mom. Very original." I roll my eyes at her, which I know she hates.

"Up and at 'em, Roman," she says, ignoring my sarcasm. "We have a lot to do today, including a birthday lunch at Chipotle, if you get up and dressed right now."

I can never resist a good burrito, so I haul my ass out of bed and throw on jeans. Yesterday, I registered for classes at North Plains High School. So now, I have to spend my fifteenth birthday school-supply shopping with Mom and getting ready to go to a new high school, six weeks after the school year started and where everybody already has their friends and a place to sit at lunch. I am not thinking about baseball and definitely not about the Dodgers today.

After we load up on school supplies, I sit on a chair near Target's fitting rooms for twenty minutes, playing *Temple Run* on my phone, while Mom scours the sale racks for clothes I can wear to school. I approve a pair of long, blue-plaid shorts and one T-shirt, a green one with an image of a mountain trail that says "Get Lost."

"You know you can't wear that shirt on your first day," Mom says.

"I'm not an idiot, Mom."

She laughs. "Come on. Let's get you fed."

While a steak burrito with extra guac isn't a fair substitute for missing the Dodger game, I'm happily stuffed by the time Mom pulls into the driveway at Grandma and Grandpa's. I carry the haul up the deck stairs and push open the door to head into the kitchen.

"Let me give you a birthday kiss," Grandma says. She is standing at the kitchen counter, leafing through the day's mail. I drop a bag full of notebooks and pens to oblige her.

Just then my phone starts to buzz. Sebastian's name appears on the display.

"Sorry, Grandma. Gotta get this."

I walk through the kitchen and plop my butt down awkwardly onto the gray, modular living room sofa as I answer the phone.

"Hey!" I say as I try to sink into the thin cushion and extend my legs over the glass coffee table.

"Hey, dude. My mom wanted me call. I was gonna text you, but she says, No. Call. So, um, happy birthday. What's going on?"

"It sucks out here, that's what. I can't wait to come back. We can shoot hoops and hit the beach."

"Yeah, totally," Sebastian says.

"What am I missing, besides the most awesome birthday baseball game?" I ask.

Wanting to keep the connection to my friends in L.A. strong, I need to keep this conversation going. Seeing my mom walk into the room, I quickly swing my legs onto the carpet and head toward the stairs and the privacy of my room, while Sebastian continues to update me.

"School sucks. My parents are pains in the ass, always getting on me to do my homework. But lunch is good—like ten of us have claimed this one table that's outside. And in gym, we're doing climbing wall."

"What are people saying? Do they ask about me?"

"Well, some people have been brutal on your mom. And now I don't have anyone in hoops to pass to. You know, Alex can't shoot! Will you come back soon?"

I laugh. That's true. Alex has one move—layups, and even those he only makes half the time.

"I'm trying," I say. "Save me a seat at the table. My mom's waiting for all this crap with Kirk to die down or something."

"Got it. Well, happy birthday. See ya."

My phone display goes black as Sebastian ends the call. I lean back against the wall outside my bedroom door, grasping tightly at the lifeline to my L.A. life.

It's just wrong I'm not sitting around that lunch table in the sunshine. I can picture Logan spending twenty minutes trying to pick up a grape with two straws. Marni going on about what ridiculous thing *just* happened on *The Bachelor*. Sam and Jack trying to get us all to meet over the weekend at Costco for a game of hide-and-seek.

Later that night, I sit at the dining room table, full from my second helping of lasagna. Mom made me my favorite meal: meat lasagna, garlic bread, and no vegetable, plus whipped up her specialty dessert from a box, Ghirardelli brownies. My grandparents and mom sing a so-terribly-off-tune-it's-funny "Happy Birthday."

Blowing out the candles on my brownie cake, I make my wish. I can't share what it is or it'll never come true, but you probably can guess. I mean what would you wish for in my shoes?

CHAPTER ELEVEN

"There's no such thing as bad publicity."

Mom tells Grandpa and me this as we sit at the kitchen table, eating grilled cheese sandwiches and slurping tomato soup.

It's turning out to be a perfectly lazy Sunday. I learn that this tabloid scandal is putting Mom out there in the spotlight. Her agent tells her, she says, this is her "fifteen minutes of fame," and she has to "strike now while she's hot."

After Mom leaves the room, Grandpa winks at me. "It's a crazy world we live in. People want to see more of your mom now that she's known for breaking up a Hollywood marriage."

I'm just glad Mom is acting more like herself again and heading back to L.A. tomorrow to powwow with her agent. Her moping around the house in yoga pants was getting old. My grandparents keep talking about how worried they are, and I was starting to agree with them.

Tomorrow is my first day at my new school. Grandma tells me I have to put on my happy face. Ugh, she's too corny. And Grandpa says I should join a team or something, to meet students who "share my interests."

In L.A., I played basketball almost every day. Kirk has this sick basketball court—a rubber-floored outdoor court with the Lakers' logo on it. I never joined a team in middle school, because there were so many things I wanted to do in L.A., like skateboard or hang out with my friends at the beach. But here there isn't so much I want to do, so I think I'm going to try out for the freshman basketball team and hopefully make a friend.

I sure could use one right now.

CHAPTER TWELVE

"There's my Tiger," Grandpa Marty announces, referring to the school mascot, as I walk into the kitchen for my first day at North Plains High School. I'm wearing a Lakers jersey, board shorts, and flip-flops. "Looking good there, Roman."

I bet he's thinking I don't realize it's twenty degrees colder here than L.A. I do, but I just don't care to adapt. It's like admitting defeat.

"I'm microwaving your oatmeal. Grandma's doing her morning meditating, and then she'll be right down."

As I sit at the kitchen table, I hear Mom talking into her phone. She enters the room and smiles at me as she ends her call and sits in the chair next to mine.

Grandpa sets a piping-hot bowl of oatmeal in front of me.

"Thanks, Grandpa." I pick up my spoon and dig in.

"Honey, remember I told you I need to run out to L.A. for a few days, to tie up some loose ends and meet with my agent? I will be back as soon as I can," Mom says. "Good luck with school. You'll do great! I will call you tonight and want to hear about all of it then."

As she rises from her seat, I decide not to stand to hug her good-bye. I'm not ready for that olive branch. At least she finally seems *good*! Like she's back to her old Steph self, with her sparkly jewelry and too-tight, too-short everything.

Welcome to my world, where I'm happy my hippie grandma is the one taking me to school today.

"Okay, Roman, let's get a move on," Grandma says as she walks in with her sunglasses pulled up on top of her head so her brown hair flows straight down her back. Unlike Mom, she doesn't wear makeup, and I think she looks just fine without it.

My grandpa is dressed in running shorts and an old race T-shirt, with his thinning dark hair swept over a large bald spot. I give thanks that these two souls are my rocks. I can always count on my grandparents to be solid.

Then there's Mom. To borrow from Grandpa's chemistry-speak, she's, well, liquid. Like water rushing with such force it pulls everything in its wake along for the ride. Mostly over unfamiliar terrain dotted with jagged rocks, but also, I gotta admit, toward some pretty phenomenal places, too.

I finish up the oatmeal and grab my backpack.

"I guess we should do this thing then," I say, saluting Grandpa goodbye and heading out the door. Kirk would be proud of my acting ability. I can see the script notes now: *Kid picks up backpack and walks down porch stairs. Fakes happiness about going to new school.*

CHAPTER THIRTEEN

North Plains High School is a towering mass of brick that takes up a whole block. It's massive. Grandma pulls up to the curb outside the main entrance, while other cars pull in and out in quick succession around us as students jump from vehicles and head into the one open front door. A security guard stands there, greeting students.

Grandma puts the car in park and turns to face me. "Grandson, one of my heroines, Eleanor Roosevelt, has a principle that I live by, and I want you to remember it whenever life get tough." She leans in closer with a serious look in her eyes. "Do one thing every day that scares you."

I nod and haul up my backpack from the car floor. "Okay, Grandma. Don't worry. I've got this." As I jump out and slam the door, I try to convince myself that's true. I wrap the black cord with my student ID over my neck and cruise past the security guard, caught in a wave of action as students yell out and then dart around me to connect with friends who are also heading inside.

The hallways are a jam-packed mess to walk down, with groups of kids crowding around lockers as they laugh, flirt, and text.

After checking in at the registration office and picking up my books, I have my schedule, a four-page map of the school showing each floor, and my new locker combination. A student I stop in the hallway points me in the direction of my first class.

Here it goes.

I've never been so confused. I rush in just after the bell to every class, lost in the maze of four floors. Room numbers jump from 307 to, turning the hallway, room 352.

"You'll get used to it," I hear a hundred times as I show my schedule to hall monitors and stop students to ask them which way is which.

Sliding into my seat in each class, I look around at so many unfamiliar faces. Almost always, the girls sitting near me introduce themselves and ask me where I'm from. But when I tell them I'm just visiting the school until I can get back to my home in L.A., they cut the conversation short and turn away to talk with their friends.

I told Mom I wanted to buy lunch the first day. I don't want to be the dorky new student with an apple and PB&J. For my Period-5 lunch, I walk into what's called the Freshman Caf. Students are standing in four different lines, so I choose the shortest. Turns out it's the line for the salad bar. Luckily, they have a cheesy pasta salad option, but my mouth waters at kids walking around with good-looking sandwiches and burgers on their trays. Carrying my pasta salad and water, I slide across from some kid sitting alone at the end of a long table.

"Hey where's the soda?" I ask.

"Are you kidding? They don't sell pop here anymore. Are you new or something?"

I tell him how I live in California and explain, while I'm at the school for now, really, I'm just passing through.

"You had pop at your school? That's awesome," he says. "Our cookies used to be so good—the grease would just collect under the plates. But now our cookies suck. I think all this health shit started because of Michelle Obama. That's what someone said, at least. Her healthy eating propaganda has all these adults brainwashed."

I laugh and introduce myself. He tells me his name is Peter, and we sit and shoot the shit until the bell rings, but we don't really hit it off. His jam is karate and Japanese club. Still, I'd like to walk with him toward my biology class, wherever the hell that is.

"Man, this place is a twisted maze," I say. "I'm headed to Room 201."

Peter laughs and points me in the mostly right direction. "I'm headed this way," and takes off in the opposite direction, leaving me stranded and clueless.

CHAPTER FOURTEEN

Here, the school day ends at 3:04. So, before I know it, I'm back in Grandma's car after spending seven hours finding my classes and feeling like a pinball as I navigated hallways with kids spilling out of classrooms in a mass exodus. My brain is fried from learning teachers' names and then having them give me a ridiculous amount of homework that is all due this week.

Names of students I met swim in my head. I think a kid named Randall and I could be friends. He's in my biology class and the only other kid I saw wearing a basketball T-shirt. Chicago Bulls, though I can live with that. But do I have to? Is this my school now? Or is Mom going to realize any day that this idea to move us back here was a bad one? Maybe she'll get a good gig going, and I'll be back in L.A. next week.

School is school, I know. That's what adults believe, at least. Kids, teachers, classes. But Chicago is no L.A., and my grandparents' house is no palace. I decide I'm going to ramp up my acting and go all-out unhappy. That's the only way I'm getting out of here.

"It's not going to work out, Grandma," I announce as I jump into her Prius after surviving Day 1 at North Plains High School. "I want to be in school there, not here. Can you talk sense into Mom?"

"How are your classes?" she asks, ignoring my question.

"Grandma. I. Want. To. Move. Back." I repeat each word as a sentence, so Grandma can't ignore the only thing I care about. "I tried this new school, but it's not for me, really."

"Roman, let's make this work, okay?"

"Grandma, no. I have a perfectly good school and friends already."

"You know I was waiting for your mom to talk to you about this. But Roman, I am going to tell you this now, so you don't get your hopes up. Your mom could never afford to move back into the school district you were in. It's over with her and Kirk. It's time for your mom to live in the real world."

"But she could—"

"What? Get a big part and become a movie star?"

We both know that won't happen. Especially now that Kirk probably blackballed her from landing any movie role.

Grandma turns her attention to the cars streaming by us as she pulls away from the curb and jabbers away, making small talk. My head is a mile behind her, processing this information she's thrown at me. After the car slows to a stop in the driveway, I open the car door and run into the house, up to my quasi-bedroom. I shut the door, throwing my backpack on the ground as I try to absorb Grandma's advice.

I guess that means my life is getting real now, too.

I need to talk to someone who understands where I'm coming from. That used to be Kirk. Before I can think it through, I grab my cell phone and dial his number. It goes to his voice mail, and I hang up without leaving a message.

I punch in a quick text.

Hey. Went to school today out here. I may play freshman basketball.

I read over the text. I want Kirk to believe I'm getting along okay. I miss him.

A few minutes later, my phone pings. Kirk has texted back.

That's my champ. You'll make a good go of it. Keep your chin up.

I don't really get what he means. Is it a basketball thing to keep my chin up?

At least I know I still have Kirk in my corner.

CHAPTER FIFTEEN

It's day four at North Plains High School. Mom called again last night from L.A. and asked me a nauseating number of questions about school. I gave her one- or two-word answers to each one.

Then she told me she auditioned for a pilot, some unoriginal comedy about an engaged couple who move in together, but he has a dog and she has a cat and the animals hate each other. Stupid, right?

I think about Grandma's mantra—no fear—as I walk up to Mrs. Landau before my first science lab.

"Um, do you think I could be lab partners with Randall?" I ask. I have met lots of dorky kids, lots of different kids, but nobody I want to hang with, so I decide to take control of the situation.

"Sure, Roman. You can jump into his group. He's with Mary and Jorge."

I walk over to where Randall and two other students are standing behind a long, black table.

"I'm Roman."

"Oh, you're new, right?" asks the girl, who has a friendly smile and unruly curly brown hair. Then she glances down at the flip-flops on my feet and introduces herself as Mary. My other new lab partner gives me his name, too.

The next forty minutes pass in science torture. Our biology lab project is dissecting chicken eggs. I step back as Jorge and Mary take charge. Randall slides a few steps over to stand next to me.

"Are you on the basketball team?" I ask him, craning my head. He is at least three inches taller than I am, although I'm taller than a lot of the freshman guys here.

"I will be. Freshman tryouts are in a few weeks. You trying out?"

"Yes, definitely." I catch myself. "If I'm still living here, I am."

The next thing I know, we're talking about Steph Curry and our shared disinterest in dissecting anything ever. Soon, we've swapped cell numbers and are making plans to shoot hoops after school.

I text Grandma I'll be home later, and, after the bell rings, I meet Randall at the school's little gym to play pickup. I'm the only white guy in the room, which is a big switch from my basketball buds in Calabasas. I head over to where an Asian kid is warming up with the ball, and he introduces himself as Daniel.

I soon discover I'm completely schooled. They are quicker than I am and can jump way higher. Daniel plays point guard, and I immediately can see he's skilled. With him on our team, we mop the floor against some tough competition. Most of my teammates' three-point shots are so pure, the ball hardly touches the rim.

I start slow, but after I warm up, I hit my stride and pull off some gritty defense moves that prove I know my way around the court.

The sweat has soaked into my socks. It feels so good being out in the cool air as I walk to Grandma and Grandpa's. That's something I didn't do much of in L.A.—walk to get somewhere.

In this town, I don't need anyone to drive me around, it's so small. But fricking cold. I'm going to wear that stupid puffy coat my grandpa got me at Old Navy and walk to school and back every day.

CHAPTER SIXTEEN

After our basketball game, I get home in no time and run up the porch steps and into the house. On my way to the fridge to grab a snack, I almost bump into Mom sitting at the kitchen table, cupping a mug of tea in her hands.

"Roman!" She jumps out of the chair and rushes to give me a hug. "I wanted to surprise you. Tell me all about high school."

I grab a vanilla pudding cup and some Oreos. Sitting at the table, I scoop up pudding with the cookies and catch Mom up on school. My English teacher, Mr. Katz, is totally L.A. cool and recites Shakespeare from memory. I'm going to start volleyball in gym soon. I tell her about Randall and basketball.

"Are we moving back soon, Mom? What's the plan?"

"I'm going to get us back to L.A., I promise. There are fresher scandals than mine for people to obsess over now. It's just I don't have a paycheck yet to do it."

She grabs a glossy piece of paper from the counter and slaps it on the table. It's an ad with her and a guy each holding their pet; the animals are growling at each other. The word *Doggone*? is plastered at the bottom of the page.

"I got the part! I play the lead in this new show. I'm heading back to L.A. next week to shoot four pilot episodes. Your grandparents and I think the most important thing is for you to finish out the school year here, and I will get us settled. Grandma told me she explained to you we can't stay in the same school district. I'll do my best to find you a school that has what you want— well, what you need."

"Four episodes?" I ask. "What happens after that?"

"Well, hopefully we'll get picked up for the full season." Mom must be able to tell I'm deflated by this news. She puts her hand gently on my arm. "It's just a year here. Think of it like a Midwest adventure."

"Mom, I have a lot of homework." I snatch up my backpack and head for the stairs. "If this doesn't work out, I hope you have a plan."

I think about what Grandma said—Mom needing to face reality. Hollywood is not real. I've learned that from living just these few weeks outside the glitter of it all.

If my fate hangs on this stupid show, *Doggone?*, I may be stuck here forever.

CHAPTER SEVENTEEN

The truth is I'm better at volleyball than I am at basketball. But I think basketball is infinitely cooler. The long shorts, the Lakers, five guys all jumping for the same ball within a two-foot area. When I see my gym schedule has me starting volleyball and badminton, I'm psyched. I don't mind slipping on the school's baggy navy-and-orange uniform.

So, it's to my supreme disappointment I walk into the gym and see badminton nets set up all around. The gym teacher, Ms. G, points me to a court where a girl is trying to balance the handle of the badminton racket on her outstretched palm. She has pink streaks in her blond hair and three tiny earrings lining each ear. I stand across from her and try the same maneuver.

"Zuzu," she says quickly, after our rackets both fall to the ground, clattering together.

I introduce myself as two students line up across the net from us. I meet Ryan and recognize Darcy from English class. At the net, the four of us make small talk through the mesh. Darcy asks how I'm liking it here so far.

I shrug my shoulders. "It's okay."

Zuzu is a sophomore. Her "real" name is Zuzana, and she moved here from Poland when she was six.

After a few minutes, Darcy pipes up. "So, I'm trying out for the badminton team. I need you guys to help me practice, okay?"

The three of us realize this badminton class has gotten serious. There's no goofing around.

"Sure, Darcy. I'm up for that," I say. Ryan and Zuzu nod their assent. We take our places on the court.

Zuzu and I grab our rackets from the ground. She's a bit shorter than me, with spindly arms and legs, so I'm not too hopeful she has an athletic bone in her body.

"Let's show her what tough opponents look like," Zuzu says to me. Darcy serves her the shuttlecock with impressive precision. Zuzu slaps it with her racket, sending it back over the net with great force. It zooms right past Darcy's racket and lands softly at her feet.

Game on!

CHAPTER EIGHTEEN

"So, why'd you move here?" Zuzu asks as we walk to our classes after gym.

"It's complicated," I respond. I still haven't figured out what I want to share with people here in Chicago, but I know my mom's whole deal is not going to be part of it.

"When's your lunch?"

We figure out we don't have the same lunch period, but we realize she lives six blocks away from my grandparents, so we make plans to walk home after school.

"I want to hear what's so complicated," she says. "My life's no picnic, either."

After the school bell rings, we meet up and walk down Lake Street, our coats zipped up to our chins against the afternoon chill. I start talking and don't want to stop. It feels freeing to tell someone about my world's tectonic shift.

After we arrived in Chicago, Grandma convinced Mom I needed to go to a therapist to talk about the sudden "disruption to my chakras," as she called it. Mom took me to see an older man, Mr. Thomas, who had hairs growing out of his ears. He asked me probing questions I had little interest in answering. I didn't need another adult telling me what to think or not to think.

After that one session, I walked back into the waiting room where Mom was reading *People* magazine and announced, "Mom, that was so useless. Don't take me back here." And she didn't.

Talking to Zuzu is different. It feels cathartic.

Leaving out the drama about my mom and the magazine, I tell Zuzu the PG version of how I ended up sleeping on a pullout sofa at my grandparents' house.

"So, you never met your dad?" she asks in amazement. "Have you Facebook stalked him?"

"My mom really hasn't told me much about him. He's a French guy named Marcel. To be honest, I kind of felt like Kirk was my dad for so long, I didn't think about it."

"Can I Facebook stalk him for you?"

I laugh. "No. Don't. But maybe one day I'll want you to."

As we round the corner near Zuzu's house, she starts pouring out her story. We sit on her cold concrete front step, our breath making puffs of white smoke in the cold air, and she tells me about her dad, who lives in Indiana and works the blackjack tables on riverboats. About how sometimes he comes home for a weekend or even a week, but mostly it's just Zuzu, her mom, and her little brother, Pawel.

"Every blue moon or so, he comes back here. And there're not many of those. As Mom tells it, my dad loves the riverboat casino life a lot and likes being a dad only a little. Though, every June, we do all road trip to Disney World for a week. I've been there eleven times."

"Wow, that's a ton," I say, thinking how weird that is. I lived, like, thirty minutes away from Disneyland in L.A. for almost ten years and went only four times, for one day each.

She shrugs. "It's their thing, I guess."

"Could be worse."

"Definitely."

The wind whips around us.

"I gotta get home. Too much algebra from Mrs. Hines," I say, unsure how to respond to her family drama but amazed I just opened up about my own so fully to someone I just met. "See you in gym tomorrow."

As I walk to my grandparents', I feel a calm I haven't had in a while. Like a heaviness I've been carrying around has lifted from my shoulders. I look forward to putting on my sweaty gym uniform tomorrow and seeing Zuzu.

If you'd told me my favorite thing about high school would be a Polish girl with pink hair, I would have said you were crazy.

CHAPTER NINETEEN

Life settles into a routine that's very different than the one I had in L.A. Since I made the freshman basketball team, I have a huge group of guys to hang out with at lunch, including Randall. Between basketball practice after school and homework, my days are packed full.

Zuzu and I text and hang out a lot. It turns out we listen to the same alternative music on Spotify and have seen every episode of *How I Met Your Mother* at least three times. We can talk for hours about everything that's good and bad in our lives. Zuzu gushes to me daily about the different guys she likes. Mostly, it's some senior named Avery, who's in her psych class.

Randall's mom drives me home from basketball practice every day. Even though it's out of their way, she insists on doing it. Mom has finished taping her four TV episodes and is helping Grandma at the food pantry while she waits to hear if *Doggone?* gets picked up by a network.

Three weeks after the start of basketball practice, I walk into the kitchen and find Grandpa at the kitchen table, reading the newspaper.

"Oh good, you're home. Do you have a lot of homework today?" he asks.

"Always, Grandpa. Why? What's up?"

"We're supposed to get a big snowstorm tonight. I told your mom I'd take you to get snow boots and gloves. Do you have time?"

I shrug. "Do I have a choice?" From the pantry I pull out a cereal box and pour myself a big bowl of Honey Nut Cheerios. Grandpa grabs the milk for me from the fridge.

"No, Grandpa. I need the other milk." I take a small chocolate milk from the side drawer of the fridge and pour that in. "No judgment. This is how we do it in L.A."

Okay, I made that part up, but it does shut down any response. After downing my snack, we are off to turn me into a Sherpa.

"How's it going at school?" Grandpa asks as he drives me to Target.

"Everything's so different," I answer, thinking about how I've changed states, schools, friends, and homes. "I guess it's okay. I don't hate it here."

He chuckles. "Well, good. That's good to know. We can make that our baseline." Grandpa relates everything to science.

"The basketball coach, Mr. Williams, is tough, though. I don't know if I'll get off the bench. Can you come to my first game on Tuesday night?"

"Sure, pal. Wouldn't miss that. We'll all be there."

"Great. I mean, I may not play, so can you explain that to Mom and Grandma? They don't have to come, if they don't want."

As we drive home in the dark with my new snow boots, we stop to pick up a pizza for dinner. Its warmth and aroma are irresistible.

"I'm starved. Can I have a piece?" I ask as we settle back into his Ford Fusion. Despite clocking more than 100,000 miles, his little red car always looks shiny and clean inside and out.

While I eat, grease dripping onto my coat, Grandpa tells me I have to give up the bedroom for a blow-up mattress in the den for a few days. My Uncle Jason is coming to stay at the house with his wife, Kathy, and their kids, Molly and Drew, for Thanksgiving.

I try to remember how old they are now... Was Molly just in kindergarten last year? Or was that the year before? How much older is Drew than Molly? Maybe two years? Three? Whatever it is, they're cute kids. I don't even mind that Drew likes to hang all over me and Molly always wants me to read to her. I know it's only for a few days.

"No problem, Grandpa. I love seeing Uncle Jason and my little cousins. Giving up the sofa bed is no problem."

CHAPTER TWENTY

Thanksgiving dinner includes almost all of my favorite foods, so I always eat too much. This Thanksgiving is no exception.

After my little cousins go to bed, I sit in the living room across from my Uncle Jason and Aunt Kathy, stuffed to the max.

Jason looks a lot like my Italian grandpa, skinny and tall, but he never got into running or any sports at all. He's in advertising, selling clients' commercials to run on television. Kathy has the whitest smile you'll ever see—it'll knock you over if you're not ready for it, which makes sense, since she manages a dental practice. Their kids are super-blond, just like Kathy, so it's funny how my Uncle Jason, with his jet-black hair, always looks like he doesn't belong in their family pictures.

Both Jason and Kathy ask question after question about how I've adjusted to living here in Chicago. I fill them in, and Jason gives me props for managing so well. Then Kathy says she's going to read and heads out of the room. I take her place on the sofa, and Jason and I flip around the free movie choices until we land on one we can agree on, the original *Rocky*. I've never seen it. For the rest of the weekend, Jason calls me Champ. That's Kirk's nickname for me, too, but I don't know how to tell Jason that.

While I am hanging out, watching TV with Uncle Jason, Mom sits with my grandparents in the next room, locked into a serious conversation. I can tell something has changed in her life and that means also in mine.

The next afternoon, Uncle Jason and his family head back to Milwaukee, and I make up an epic plate of Thanksgiving leftovers. As I sit at the table in stuffing heaven, Mom slides over to sit next to me.

"Well, that was our first Chicago Thanksgiving in a while," she says. "I really enjoyed it. I hope you did, too."

I grunt in agreement and shove more potatoes into my mouth as I wait for Mom's big announcement.

"Honey. I do have some news about *Doggone*? It doesn't look like it will get picked up by a network. My agent isn't too hopeful about it at least."

"Shocking!" I answer while thinking, *Not*!

"Yes, well, I had an interesting experience on the set. When we were getting ready to go on camera for the final episode, our makeup artist, Lena, went into premature labor, and we had to call an ambulance. It was all really scary. She's fine, she has a baby girl now. But, anyway, I ended up doing my makeup and also the makeup of two of my costars for the show."

"Okay, Mom. Thanks for sharing how you saved the day."

"Roman, listen. I was good at it. And I liked it. So, I looked into going back to school to become a makeup artist. I think it just makes sense for me. I could get a steady job and not have to worry about auditioning and all. That isn't working out for me so well."

I laugh. Maybe disaster is the word I would use.

"I found a great program in L.A. where I can get experience pretty much right away, but it'll mean at least a year of full-time school. Some of it I can take online.

"Are you all right living here with your grandparents until the end of the school year? I'll still come back tons, and we can do FaceTime every day, if that's okay. I'll bunk in with Traci and her boyfriend for a few weeks, until I can get my own place. Her boyfriend has a car he's letting me use, because he has a company car, too."

"Sounds like you decided already, Mom."

I want to lay the guilt on thick. I'm caught off-guard. This is not the conversation I expected us to have. But I'm also relieved. I realize she is working harder on this stability thing because of me.

I figure, if she is making an attempt to adapt, then I can, too. "Mom, I'm okay here… for now. You should go for it," I say. And I mean it.

Finally! My mom has a plan and I think it's a good one.

The afternoon before Mom leaves for L.A., she comes to watch my basketball game. I kinda mess up. I'm half a beat slow in my passes, and it shows. Daniel's our point guard, and after two of his bullet passes go off my hands out of bounds during the first quarter, I've lost some of his confidence and the coach pulls me out. I'm annoyed with myself as I realize the team doesn't trust me too much after that.

The coach puts me back in late in the third quarter, and I somewhat redeem myself with tough defense and a few good plays. But I walk off the court pissed that my offensive skills come up short.

We lose by five lousy points.

Mom then takes me and three of my teammates—Randall, Jordan, and Malcolm—out for Mexican food. Big mistake. They sit squashed into a booth across from us with moony eyes as they hang on her every word. They're completely captivated being in her presence.

I'm sure they know she's more infamous than famous in Hollywood as, in between chomping on chips and salsa and beef tacos, they ask seemingly innocent questions about actors she has met and movies she has been in. I'm not clueless. I know the whole messy drama of why we left L.A. has trickled down from parent to child and spread stealthily around the community.

"I'll miss you," Mom says the next morning in the kitchen, suitcase by her side.

"Yeah," I say as she envelops me in a hug.

"I'm so glad you have such nice friends. It was great getting to talk with them last night," she adds.

I love my mom but oh man, can she be self-absorbed. I can't stay mad at her. It's just who she is.

I mean, honestly, Mom and my friends spent the whole dinner talking about boring Hollywood stuff. She does not realize how confusing it is to have all those memories churn up again. It reminds me of when every day was golden and the hardest thing I ever had to think about was if Alex and I should fire up *Call of Duty* or *Grand Theft Auto* on my PlayStation.

CHAPTER TWENTY-ONE

December is the second craziest month I have ever had, and that's only because my September was so life-shattering. Teachers don't care that you have basketball and chores, friends and video games. They don't even care you have to study for finals. They are busy handing out reading assignments, worksheets, papers, and group projects like they're candy. I'm up to my eyeballs in homework the minute I get home from basketball.

One night, I'm being lulled to sleep by Ms. Hines's equations when my phone rings, jolting me back into consciousness. The word *Kirk* lights up the screen. I press the button to talk before I have time to think.

"Hi, Champ! It's Kirk," I hear right away.

"Yeah, hi," I answer, feeling nervous and excited.

"So, I had some time, wanted to see how you're getting along."

"I'm good. I'm playing on the freshman basketball team. Scored six points last game."

"That's great," he answers. "I hear you're coming to L.A. to visit your mom for Christmas. I feel terrible. Our movie is filming in Atlanta right now. I won't be in L.A. for another month."

"That's okay." Secretly, I'm just thrilled he wants to see me and, I think, even misses me a little bit.

"Your mom called and told me she's going back to school. We talked about you mostly. It sounds like you're doing really well. Even though your mom and I are in the past, I hope the two of us can stay in touch. I want to hear what you're up to. Promise?"

"Yes, sure. I promise. Thanks, Kirk."

"No problem. Keep me in the loop, Champ. Have a great Christmas."

"Yeah, you, too."

When we hang up, I find myself completely revived and ready to tackle math head-on. Maybe even read a chapter in biology.

CHAPTER TWENTY-TWO

The day my winter school break begins, I fly out to visit Mom for a week, knowing nothing will be the same about L.A. ever again. She picks me up at the airport in a borrowed Nissan. When Mom pulls into the parking lot of her one-bedroom rental in Sherman Oaks, it is far from our lives in Calabasas in so many ways. She's already warned me I'm sleeping on a pull-out sofa in the living room.

"The building has a pool," she says, pointing ridiculously to a fenced-in area with an oval pool bordered by concrete and a smattering of plastic reclining chairs. It's like trying to sugarcoat spinach… It just doesn't work.

The sofa bed in Mom's small apartment is even less comfortable than the one at my grandparents' house, so that's super-fun. Thankfully, the weather is perfect, and I meet my friends at the beach almost every day. I pick up right where things left off with Sebastian and Alex, though my mom stays in the car whenever she drives me to hang out. I can tell she's still embarrassed.

When I mention to her that Troy is taking me out to lunch the next day, she makes no effort to hide her disgust. She looks about to blow her top. Then, an hour before Troy is supposed to come pick me up, she makes up some lame-o excuse about having to do a bunch of errands.

Troy comes by the apartment to take me out for a burger and gives me a Christmas card from Kirk with two $100 bills inside and a huge tin of homemade cookies from Cora.

My lunch with Troy feels so weird. That's because, the whole time we're doing the small-talk thing, I can't shake what Mom says he did.

I get it. Troy's not stupid. Kirk's his boss, not Mom. Still, if it's true, Mom didn't deserve the outing he gave her.

We celebrate Christmas at Traci's new home. She bought it with her fiancé, Len, and they have a dog named Copper and a Christmas tree all decorated with ornaments and white lights. There's even a Christmas stocking with my name on it filled with candy.

"Keep digging," Traci says as I pull out a motherlode of Twix, gum, Snickers, and Twizzlers. At the bottom, I locate an Apple gift card.

"Sweet! Thanks," I say. Then Mom gives me her gift, Beats headphones.

"Wow, this is great. I needed these both big-time."

I hand Mom a small wrapped box, a pair of silver hoop earrings, each with a dangling crystal. I picked them out with Zuzu in Oak Park. She puts them on right away, the silver gleaming through her dark hair.

"Pretty," Traci says as Mom pulls out the mirror from her purse.

She holds it in front of her face and stares at her reflection for a few seconds.

"Yes, I love them," she finally decides as she tilts her head from side to side.

I present Len and Traci with a plastic bag filled with some of Cora's cookies. Len opens it and passes cookies around, while Copper comes over and snatches one from Len's outstretched hand then runs away to devour it.

These presents are more fun than the Gap shopping spree Grandma and Grandpa took me on as their Christmas gift before I left for L.A.

In the car heading to the airport at the end of the week, I am pleased Mom is wearing the dangling earrings I got her. I realize she doesn't have one other sparkle on her body, though. Nothing shiny or glittery stuck onto her shoes, top, or pants. In fact, during the whole week she wore kinda muted things. Like *mom* clothes.

"See you soon, Sport," she says as we stand outside the car. "Be good for your grandparents. Love you." She hugs me tightly. After a few seconds, I move away to grab my suitcase from the open trunk. This time, leaving L.A. is not quite so hard.

CHAPTER TWENTY-THREE

On the last morning of the year, Grandma makes me her special wheat-germ pancakes, which aren't as bad as they sound because of all the syrup I pour on them. She asks me to reflect on this past year and "its blessings."

Well, I can tell you this. These are just some of the experiences I'm proud I survived this year:

No longer living with Kirk or Cora and Troy!

Snow!

Moving into my grandparents' house!

New school!

Sitting on the bench half the season! (But then, getting off the bench and scoring twenty-nine points in five games!)

Leaving my L.A. friends!

Dissecting a chicken leg in biology… Gross!

I spend New Year's Eve hanging out with Zuzu at a party with her friends from this school club she's part of called Spoken Word. The kids in it are really cool. Louder and different than anyone from my life in L.A.

Confession: I kinda like them, even though, when the clock struck midnight, they pulled me into one of their goofy group hugs.

CHAPTER TWENTY-FOUR

January is miserable. I wonder why anybody would live here on purpose. Every morning, I zip up my coat, put on heavy-ass gloves, and force myself to step into the deep freeze, following the white puffs of my breath as I walk to school and keeping an eye out for patches of ice.

Today, our English teacher, Mr. Katz, introduces us to a guest speaker, Mr. Collins. He stands in front of our class wearing metallic-blue eyeglasses, his blond hair pulled into a bun on top of his head. He wears a purple-and-white plaid shirt with rolled-up cuffs dotted with purple polka dots. Surprisingly, this odd contrast works.

"It's great to be here today. I run North Plains' Spoken Word club. We have about fifty students who come to our meetings at any one time. We meet Tuesdays and Thursdays after school in Room 330 to read, write, and perform poetry. I visit each freshman English class to give our students a sense of what we do at Spoken Word. So, I hope you're ready to jump into this world of free-form poetry with me for the next forty minutes."

He stands square in the middle of the room and says he's going to read us something called an "anti-ode." I feel like he's speaking to me when he asks, "Is there anyone who moved to the Midwest from somewhere else?"

A few hands go up, and Mr. Collins points to them. The students announce, "New York," "Sarasota," "Venezuela," "St. Louis," "Trinidad."

Darcy says, "Roman *just* moved here."

Twenty-five pairs of eyes turn to face me. I croak, "California."

"Okay, great. Well, this anti-ode I'm going to read is a good example of something that is sarcastic, not serious. Something the writer is praising but not really praising. I think you'll have fun with this."

And then he begins in a strong, steady voice:

Ode to the Midwest
By Kevin Young

> *The country I come from*
> *Is called the Midwest.*
>
> > —*Bob Dylan*

I want to be doused
in cheese

& fried. I want
to wander

the aisles, my heart's
supermarket stocked high

as cholesterol. I want to die
wearing a sweatsuit—

I want to live
forever in a Christmas sweater,

a teddy bear nursing
off the front. I want to write

a check in the express lane.
I want to scrape

my driveway clean

myself, early, before
anyone's awake —

that'll put em to shame —
I want to see what the sun

sees before it tells
the snow to go. I want to be

the only black person I know.

I want to throw
out my back & not

complain about it.
I wanta drive

two blocks. Why walk —

I want love, n stuff —

I want to cut
my sutures myself.

I want to jog
down to the river

& make it my bed —

I want to walk
its muddy banks

& make me a withdrawal.

I tried jumping in,
found it frozen—

I'll go home, I guess,
to my rooms where the moon

changes & shines
like television.

He stands silently as we absorb the words and their twisted meaning. Honestly, my mind is blown. I am so tired of reading Shakespeare and books by long-dead people like the one we just finished, *Of Mice and Men.* Hearing something this weird and irreverent is awesome!

"Claire," Mr. Collins says, handing a piece of paper to a girl whose skin is the color of honey and faintly freckled, like she spent winter break sitting on a beach in Florida. "Can you read this next anti-ode by one of our own graduates, Natalie Richardson?" He adds, "Claire's older sister, Annie, is one of our star Spoken Word veterans. She competes with us in the Louder Than a Bomb competition in Chicago that we travel to each March. Claire's been to a number of our meetings. It's nice to see you today."

Claire nods, her long, blonde hair framing a pretty face lit up by a warm smile. I sit up a little straighter as she takes the paper and reads:

Fried Shrimp
for my father

Only when Mama left would you make
them, the kitchen cold with gusts of air from gaping
window and door, yellow oil bursting in cell
—like bubbles on the stove. You would have bought
the ingredients that morning: fresh shrimp from the fish
market with salted floors, lemons, good bread crumbs.
The Tabasco we'd have. Once, I de-veined the shrimp
at the sink: Motown hard and slick on the radio, your
voice slippery as palm oil. You might have been drunk.
Beneath the cold water, each shrimp swelled heavy
as your sober-lipped promise in my hands. Sharply,
I removed each blue vein—blunt as your drunkenness,
but easy to tear apart—this spine of thread, feeble
string you ask me to break again, again.

The room is quiet as we sit and think about the sad picture this poet paints of her father.

"I want you all to connect with your emotions as they rise to the surface and capture them on paper. Then, take what you've written, read it over, and go a little bit deeper," says Mr. Collins. "You want to aim to include these elements in your poem." He walks up to the white board and writes out five phrases in bold capital letters.

"You'll want to make sure there is a SPECIFIC INCIDENT, that the poem has at least two STRIKING LINES with NO CLICHÉS. Ask yourself, 'Does my poem start IN THE MOMENT? Is there SPECIFICITY?'"

Mr. Collins then turns away from the white board and stands between two desks in the middle of the room, signaling us with a nod of his head that the lesson has concluded.

Now it's our turn. Ten minutes. Write an anti-ode. I sit thinking as a million things that annoy me or are painful, upsetting, and terrible run through my brain. Suddenly, what I really want to say hits me. My pen flies across the paper.

I feel pleased with what I wrote. But when Mr. Collins asks for volunteers to read their anti-odes, no way am I doing that. Joey reads his poem about spiders. Madison reads hers about throwing up at a friend's birthday party. Samuel writes about the Black Jesus doll on his dresser.

Mr. Collins walks up to desks and puts out his hand, inviting the student sitting in front of him to share what is down on paper. I watch as he heads my way. Looking down at the words I scribbled quickly, I realize all eyes are fixed my way so I better make the best of it. That's one lesson from Kirk I'll keep with me. He never let me off the hook when I did something half-ass. His response to me always was "good isn't good enough," and I now hear his voice repeating that in my head. So, this one's for Kirk.

I offer up my anti-ode. I read it loudly and with feeling. I feel free and fierce as the words burst out from deep within:

> My butt hurt for a week.
> Black and blue all up and down my thigh.
> Moving like molasses on the court.
> My friends, they think it's funny.
> My Grandma blames Grandpa.
> He feels real bad.
> He bought me the snow boots, after all.
> But it isn't his fault.
> Nobody warned my L.A. brain about something called
>   black ice.

Laughter erupts from all corners of the room.

"Man, at first, I thought your butt hurt from a whupping," Jonas yells out. More laughter.

"That was well done," Mr. Collins says, nodding at me. "I liked your poem, but I also liked your performance. You matched your facial expressions to the words and really made us feel your pain."

I feel puffed up from the class reaction, from his praise. I slide the loose paper with hastily but intently scribbled lines back into my notebook. I'll have to show this to Zuzu—it probably will make her laugh, too.

The bell rings. Mr. Collins is standing by the door, holding a stack of flyers that he places in each kid's outstretched fingers as they head out. As I walk by, he looks square at me and presses a flyer into my hands.

"Don't forget, Room 330, Tuesdays and Thursdays. Hope to see you there."

I take the flyer and nod goodbye, realizing my nod also could be interpreted as a *yes*.

But this interpretation doesn't bother me. I quickly fold the flyer and stick it in my jeans pocket.

CHAPTER TWENTY-FIVE

"Hey, Zuzu," I say as we're sitting on the floor in her bedroom, propped up against an obnoxiously large, fuzzy, orange beanbag. It's a Saturday afternoon, and we're taking a much-deserved study break.

Zuzu is really hyper about her classes. She's got dreams of going to NYU. When she told my grandma about wanting to go there, Grandma told her that Eleanor Roosevelt thing, too.

Zuzu loves my grandma.

"Mr. Collins was in our class last week," I say. "We did Spoken Word stuff. Is that what you guys do, just write poems and read them?"

"Kinda," she answers. "We also compete. And not just solo pieces. Sometimes we perform in groups."

"You mean like team poetry? How does that work?"

"It's challenging to put individual poems together on stage," she explains. "A team needs creativity and good chemistry to pull it off."

I nod. "Competitive poetry. I'd like to try it."

"Though sometimes it's just for fun. We do a lot of sharing."

"Mr. Collins had us write a poem. It was an ode, or an anti-ode, he called it." I pull my backpack closer.

"Yeah, they're the funnest to write," she says.

"He asked some girl, Claire, to read a poem. Do you know her and her sister?"

"Sure. Annie is epic in Spoken Word. Love that girl!"

"Well, maybe I can check it out one day. Does Claire go a lot?"

Zuzu gives me a look. She knows I'm interested in more than Spoken Word.

"Sometimes. Sure. But don't you have basketball every day after school?"

"Not after January. The freshman team isn't gonna make sectionals."

"Bummer."

"Totally," I say in my very lame Valley Girl accent.

We both crack up.

"Can I show you something?" I yank my notebook from my bag. "This is what I wrote." I hand her the loose page I've been saving.

Zuzu reads it, wrapping a strand of her hair around her finger as she studies the words.

She giggles. "Yes. This is perfect. You have to come to Spoken Word. You're good. We'll have fun." She adds, "And I'll check with Annie to see if Claire's coming."

"But none of those group hugs, okay?" I say cautiously. "That was weird."

"No problem." Then she leans over and gives me a hug.

CHAPTER TWENTY-SIX

During lunch on Monday, Randall asks if I'm going to the Valentine's Dance next month.

"So that's a thing?" I ask, trying to wrap my head around the fact that there is a school dance for something as mushy as Valentine's Day.

"I asked Lauren to go with me. But you can't just ask 'em. You have to make it big."

"How big? And what'd she say?"

"Oh, I knew from Becky she was going to say yes or I wouldn't have done it. But I went to her house last night and put all these glow sticks on the front porch in the shape of a question mark. Then I rang the bell."

"Seriously? You did that?"

Randall nodded. "Her mom answered the door, and Lauren was right behind her, so that was annoying. But then her mom disappeared. Who are you asking?"

"Gotta work on that," I say, though I know who I want to ask. I just don't know how.

After surviving another school day, I find Zuzu camped out next to my locker.

"Can you come to Spoken Word tomorrow? Annie said Claire will be there this week," she says, teasing.

"Not tomorrow. Got practice. But Thursday I can. Our game's at seven."

"Cool. See you then!" She heads down the hall.

I now have an excuse to hang out with Claire. I just need intel to see if she'll go to the dance with me.

CHAPTER TWENTY-SEVEN

"You look nice," Zuzu says on Thursday just as I'm slamming my locker shut.

"Yeah? Thanks," I respond.

My everyday uniform at school is T-shirt and jeans. I did make an extra effort today—my Gap shirt has three buttons on it!

I grab my backpack and head with Zuzu to Spoken Word club. The meeting room is not just a boring classroom. It's basically a mini-auditorium with a stage below twelve rows of seats that slope up toward the door. A few students are scattered among the seats, their desks flipped up and tucked along the edges of their chairs. We grab spots near the back of the room.

Zuzu watches the flow of students until Annie walks in with Claire, who is wearing dark jeans with one ripped knee and a long-sleeved, green V-neck shirt. A silver butterfly pendant on a thin silver chain shimmers lightly around her neck.

"Annie! Over here." Zuzu motions, and they plunk down next to us.

"You're in my English class," Claire says as she leans over Zuzu to talk to me.

"Yeah. I'm Roman."

"Sure, I know. The kid from California. I'm Claire." She flashes her mega-watt smile.

Mr. Collins strides up to the white board at the front of the classroom then turns to us and bows slightly. "Today, we will be writing flash fiction. Does anybody know what that means?"

He points to a student with her hand straight up in the air in one of the front rows.

"It's telling a story but with not a lot of words."

"Yes, that's pretty much it, Gina," Mr. Collins says then turns to the whiteboard and writes:

For Sale: Baby Shoes, Never Worn.

"This has been attributed to Ernest Hemingway, one of the greatest writers of the twentieth century. It's an extreme example of a story packed into just six words. Your mission today is to write just six brilliant words that tell a story. Think about the message you want to convey and what imagery you want to represent." He adds, "I have a few other examples of flash fiction to share with you. Since it's the new year how about…?" He writes:

January resolve. February waver. March ditch.

"A friend told me about something that happened to him recently, and I realized it made for good flash fiction, though, in this case, it was not fiction and rather unfortunate." He writes on the board:

Flat Tire. New Job. No Job?

"Now, let's spend about ten minutes. I want each of you to write your own six-word story. Make each of your six words shimmer, like a brilliant piece of art."

"No pressure, right, Mr. Collins?" jokes Joey.

We bend over our desks, pens in hand, and dive down into our thoughts. The room is pure silence except for the scribbling, scratching out of phrases, and a few toes tapping.

After ten minutes pass, students start sharing their stories with Mr. Collins as he captures them on the whiteboard.

Claire's is classic:

Homework due tomorrow. Is dog hungry?

Zuzu's is real:

Turn Music Down? Maybe You're Old!

Since I'm starving, mine is easy:

Didn't plan ahead. No Food. Help!

A half hour later, Mr. Collins wraps up the meeting.

"I don't give much homework, but I want to throw out some brainwork to keep us fresh. For our next meeting, I want everyone to write a short poem with the word *devour* in it. You'll each have up to thirty seconds to perform your piece." He checks his watch and walks away, leaving me bummed out I now have something called "brainwork" to worry about.

"Are you going to these meetings now?" Claire asks as we pick up our backpacks and head into the hallway.

"I'm thinking about it. Though the homework thing is not selling it. You?"

"Yeah. He usually doesn't do that," she says, slipping her pack over her shoulders.

"That's good to know." I feel slightly reassured.

"I started going to meetings because of my sister. But it kinda grows on you. Annie really gets into the competition part in Chicago. Louder Than a Bomb. She's so good. She wanted me to make the team this year with her."

"So, did you?"

She shakes her head. "Nope. But there's always next year."

"Oh, when were the tryouts?"

"In November. You should hear how good some of the kids at our school are."

"I'm sure you're good, too."

She dips her head modestly and then looks up, captivating me with her blue eyes. They remind me of the glinting waters of the Pacific Ocean that I would surf when I lived in L.A.

"I need to find Annie—she's giving me a ride home," Claire says, hypnotizing me with a small wave goodbye.

"Sure. See you tomorrow. I think we have to read, like, fifty pages tonight for Katz."

"I'm done already." She blushes. "With the book."

"You finished it?" I blurt out. "Damn!"

Claire shrugs. "Well, to be honest, *The Kite Runner* is not easy reading. It's so sad. Good luck with it."

As we head off in different directions, my body buzzes with electricity. I force myself to shake off the message flashing in my brain, the one telling me to turn around and walk back into her world.

That will have to wait until tomorrow.

CHAPTER TWENTY-EIGHT

Sitting in study hall before Spoken Word on Tuesday, I write out a poem in fifteen minutes about being devoured by stupid homework. I read it over and think, *Genius*.

I start on my biology worksheets. Then, a few minutes before the period ends, I skim the poem I've just written and I'm not as impressed with myself. In fact, the poem kinda sucks. How did the same words go from brilliant to bad so quickly? I think about ditching Spoken Word, but of course I know I won't, because I really want to see Claire.

Filing into the club's classroom, it takes a while for everyone to quiet down so Mr. Collins can get the meeting started. I'm sitting next to Claire. Zuzu is nowhere to be found.

"I told everyone you had brainwork to bring in, an original poem using the word devour. I'm not going to call you to task if you haven't anything to recite," says Mr. Collins. "This exercise is for your benefit." I could swear he is looking at me. Now I feel stupid I was so lazy. But I also feel glad I'm off the hook. This poem is staying in my backpack and then going straight into the recycling bin. (At my grandma's house, I learned right away you dare not throw paper anywhere else.)

"If you want to read your poem, just stand up where you are now and share it. I don't expect you to have it memorized, but if you do, even better."

One by one, students pop up in their seats and read their poems. A few recite them from memory. It's pretty amazing to hear what the students all do with the same word.

Shivani reads her poem about a grandma being devoured by cancer.

Emma has memorized hers and performs it with deep emotion. It's about her family changing as her brother gets devoured by life in college.

Desmond's poem is really heavy and sad, about losing a race after feeling devoured by a racist comment made when he was running in a track meet.

Gina reads hers about being devoured by love.

Annie's poem is about being devoured by Instagram and Snapchat.

Joey reads a long poem about feeling devoured by spending fifty hours driving with his mom in the passenger seat before he can take his driver's license test.

Claire's poem is great. She reads a laundry list of feeling devoured by things she loves that aren't good for her but she can't escape, like Reese's Peanut Butter Cups and the Kardashians, plus the GroupMe messages and texts that always cause her phone to vibrate.

I am good just hanging out and listening today. I take in all the ways my classmates get devoured. Nobody who stands up is boring and reads a poem about homework, that's for sure.

Now I get it. I'll take Mr. Collins's advice next time and treat the projects he gives us like I give a damn. Because I honestly do.

CHAPTER TWENTY-NINE

The only way I may go through with my insane idea to ask Claire to the Valentine's dance is if I actually say it out loud to someone. Someone who will tell me my idea is brilliant, of course. And who better than the person whose job in life is to be the champion of all things Roman?

After I got home from L.A., Mom ramped up the calls and texts. She started adding these sad-face emojis when I didn't respond to her stupid "how are you?" messages. The next thing I know, she's landed an internship with a makeup artist who has a gig doing hair and makeup at ABC-TV in Chicago, so she's back living in Oak Park.

I figure I'll make her day, maybe even her year.

"Hey, Mom, there's this girl, Claire. I'm gonna ask her to the Valentine's Dance," I say, standing behind where she sits in the living room, watching YouTube videos of people putting on makeup. It's amazing how many hours she spends doing that.

"Claire's a lucky girl." She turns to me as she shuts the laptop.

I shake my head. That's pretty much what I was expecting her to say. She's gotten so sappy since we moved back here.

"Well, it's gonna be a big pain. The kids at school do stupid things, like one junior on the varsity basketball team asked his date to go to the dance in front of the whole school at the Spirit Assembly."

She laughs. "That sounds fun."

"It's doesn't sound fun to me. But anyway, Zuzu found out from Claire's sister that she wants me to ask her. So, now I have to make it, like, interesting."

"Yes, something dramatic. The Santis can do drama. That should be no problem."

"She's in Spoken Word, and I go sometimes. So, I was thinking of writing some poem thing and maybe reading that at the beginning of a meeting. But it would be embarrassing."

"She'd be flattered, don't you think? That you'd put yourself out there like that?"

"That's what I'm going for, I guess."

I walk away thinking, now that I've said it, there's no going back. *What have I gotten myself into?*

CHAPTER THIRTY

It drives me crazy. There are no secrets in this house. It's obvious Grandma and Grandpa are clued in that I plan to ask Claire to the dance. They give me knowing smiles that create crinkles around their eyes.

Late Saturday morning, Grandma knocks on my bedroom door. "Come in," I answer as I shut down the *Madden* game I'm playing and jump off the bed.

"Roman, your mom said you're involved with a poetry club at school. I think that's great, and I bought you a present. Something special for you to write your poems in."

She hands me a gray, leather-bound notebook. On the cover it reads in white block letters: *All our dreams can come true if we have the courage to pursue them.*

"Thanks, Grandma. I'll use this for sure." The leather feels soft. I throw the notebook onto my bed.

"I'm so glad." Her eyes follow it landing on the bed. "We'd also love to come and see you perform," she adds gently.

"Grandma, if it's okay, not yet. I'm just figuring it all out."

"Yes, that makes sense. I completely understand. You just let us know then." A bunch of my clothes lie around the floor and I know she sees them but I guess decides not to say anything about my mess. "Grandpa is making Nutella pancakes for you. Can you smell them?"

"Yes. I was hoping that's what it was. I'll be right down."

That weekend, I spend hours and hours in my bedroom, sitting on the lumpy pullout bed and staring at a blank piece of lined paper in my new leather notebook. My first, second, third, and fourth attempts at a poem litter the floor around my bed. Saturday, I load up the recycle bin with my crumpled rejects.

I realize this Spoken Word idea may not work out and begin to think about other ways I can impress Claire with an invitation to the dance. I heard about one sophomore who filled a girl's locker with ping-pong balls he had written on, asking her to the dance. But the rumor is she turned him down after all that effort anyway.

I watched one guy show up in the lunchroom with flowers, while he stammered out an invitation, but then the girl took the flowers in her hand and, with a big smile, pulled out one stem and slid it behind his ear. Then he inched closer to her as they began talking—the flower still in his ear. It was so obvious they were already dating.

Nothing pushes my current idea out of the running.

Sunday, I sleep until 11 a.m. I lie in bed, stewing over my hard work last night and the words that would not come out right.

Suddenly, I jump up with the idea of a poem floating in my head. I grab the notebook and open it to a page riddled with words. The lines are hidden under angry slashes where I crossed out crappy sentences. Pen in hand, I turn to a fresh sheet of paper, and sentence after sentence begin to pour out. I go along for the ride.

I read the words over, feeling pleased with myself, and then close the notebook to put it away. I remember how Mr. Collins says, while working on a poem, we should take a break after a solid first draft is down on paper. Later, we should go back to it and dig a little deeper. So, I do just that. Sunday night, I polish and prod it until I admit it is the best poem I can pull from my head. I'm pumped by the feeling I've written something honest and real but not mushy or anything. Now I have a few days to memorize it.

At lunchtime on Monday, I get a pass from the hall monitor and go looking for Mr. Collins. He's in the English office, working with a student. I wait, scrolling through my phone to pass the time. When Mr. Collins is finished, he motions me over.

"Hey, Mr. Collins, I was hoping for a favor. I want to ask Claire Matthews to the Valentine Dance with this poem." I thrust the paper with my typed-out poetry in front of him.

Mr. Collins slowly reads my poem. Then he reads it again. He stares at me with an expression of approval.

"Well done, Mr. Santi Are you proposing hijacking my class to read this to her?"

"Well, yeah. Sorta." I look down at my feet.

"Okay, hijack away. You're up first tomorrow. Good luck!"

Thanks," I say, looking up at him and feeling validated that this is the right move to make.

He hands me back the poem.

"Wait," I say, brushing off the fog that descended with Mr. Collins's approval. "Not tomorrow. We have our last basketball game. Thursday though?"

He pulls out his calendar and checks it quickly. "Sure, then. Thursday. We're in the writing lab that afternoon, but we'll start out in the classroom. That would work, too."

"Okay, great. See you," I say as I head back to the cafeteria. I still have fifteen minutes of freedom before the bell rings and I have to head off to my most dreaded class, biology.

CHAPTER THIRTY-ONE

"So, you and Mr. Collins are in cahoots!" Zuzu says as we walk down the hallway after school. "I love that word—cahoots."

"I guess so," I answer.

"You know you could have baked Claire a cake."

"Now you tell me." I break away from her side as we walk quickly into the Spoken Word classroom. I sit down: front row, center. Behind me in the higher seats are Claire, Annie, Zuzu, Gina, Joey, and Max.

As more kids file in. I channel my inner Hollywood. I lived there long enough and have definitely seen enough. Still, I begin to doubt if I can stand up here and recite the words I've spent more than an hour memorizing without messing up.

Then I think of my grandma and her mantras.

No Fear. I've got this.

Before I know it, I'm on.

"Okay, crew," says Mr. Collins, facing us with a serious expression plastered on his face. "Settle in. We have a student performing a special poem this afternoon. Mr. Santi. Take it away." He shifts to the left and folds himself into a seat near the corner.

I take a few steps up to the front of the room and turn toward the assembled group. I look out at the faces: confused, bored, interested. I glance over at Claire. She's tuned in at least. I'd say her expression is in the "interested" category.

My mind kicks into high gear. The words anxiously reach the tip of my tongue. I look over at Claire and then switch my gaze to a spot on the wall behind her. I open my mouth to begin.

I've tried to write lines for what I want to say
Although I'm not sure if I should
Be up here doing this today
I'm going to roll with it anyway
I have a confession I need to make
My interest in Spoken Word began partly for the sake
Of getting to hang with some peeps that rate
So, today I'm saying what I hope you think's fly
'Cause this kinda stunt is not usually my style
But here it goes
I'm following these guy rules
They say I should do somethin' snug
You know, make it all that, don't be a dud
So, I'm standing here in front of this motley club
To say something that's been stuck in my mind
I gotta ask while I still have this time
> *Claire Matthews,*
> *Will you go to the Valentine's Dance with me?*
So there, I've gone ahead and done it now
And I hope your answer is that you want to... go

After I blurt out the final syllable, I take a deep breath to slow down my heart, which is beating, beating, beating like crazy. I look over at the one person in the room I was talking to. The reason I'm standing up here.

Claire has her face buried in her hands.

Suddenly she looks up. "You're crazy!" she yells out to me, the words echoing through the room.

Oh, no. What have I done? Now I've totally made a fool of myself and of her and... I start to think about my next move... A quiet exit. Maybe a new identity.

But then Claire stands and she's laughing.

"Sure, Roman. I'll go to the dance with you," she says.

Kids clap. They make kissing noises. One mutters, *"Eeewww."* And I hear worse.

I don't care about the chatter. I did it. I survived, and now I have a date with Claire to the Valentine's Dance. *Phew*!

CHAPTER THIRTY-TWO

Our basketball season is over, but a bunch of us decide to meet up in the small gym to play pickup. I'm all in—I can use all the practice I can get, if I want to make JV next year.

Today, I don't have my basketball shoes on, just my beat-up sneakers. We start a three-on-three game, and early on I get the ball and take it down the court. I see an opening and launch a jumper, but I also come down hard on someone's foot. My right ankle twists, and searing pain shoots from my foot up through my body.

I rock back heavily on the shiny wood floor and thrust my throbbing ankle up high. Randall and Daniel rush to my side and lean down to stick their arms under mine to pick me up, helping me hop off the court. Daniel steps away and Randall lets me lean on him as we head down the hallway to the big gym. The women's volleyball coach points us to where a trainer is taping up a kid's wrist.

"Go, Randall," I say through gritted teeth after I gently lower myself onto the nearby bleachers, trying to keep pressure off my pulsing foot. "I'm fine."

"I'm not going to leave you here alone." He plunks down next to me and we wait. Fifteen agonizing minutes later, the trainer walks over.

"Hi, I'm Eric Richardson. What happened?"

Randall fills Mr. Richardson in for me after he realizes the pain from my foot has made the first few words out of my mouth pretty incoherent. Eric nods to Randall that he understands what went down, and Randall takes off, leaving us to figure out next steps.

Eric leans over my right foot and pushes and prods my sore, sorry ankle until he comes up with a diagnosis.

"Looks like you have a pretty decent sprain here. Nothing major. Let's wrap it, and, when you go home, ice it good for twenty minutes every hour until bed. Come by tomorrow before school, and I'll take another look. We'll see how your ankle responds overnight and what we need to do."

Isn't this just great? I literally just asked Claire to the dance, and now it looks like I maybe won't be dancing. I'm angry at myself, but at this point, I can't do anything except what Eric has told me—rest it, ice it.

After Eric wraps my ankle, I text Mom asking her to pick me up and then make my way to the front entrance.

The next day, Mom drops me at school an hour early so I can get looked at by the trainer and see if I'm screwed.

I'm not. Overnight, the swelling has gone down a lot. Eric tells me to take it easy, keep Ace wrapping it for the rest of the week, and take Advil or Aleve as needed. I get an elevator pass and hobble around school with a stupid bandage on my foot.

Eric was right. After four days, I'm feeling almost back. I ditch the bandage, but by the end of the day, I'm spent and my foot is hurting. I tell Mom and everyone I'm fine, which is sorta true.

CHAPTER THIRTY-THREE

Two tickets to the Valentine's Day Dance: Check
Suit and tie: Check
Corsage to match Claire's dress: Check
Date pictures at Randall's: Check

Claire looks so beautiful in her bright blue dress that matches her eyes. But she can barely walk in her ridiculous silver shoes with spiky heels. Her hair falls in loose curls around her neck, and I resist the urge to tell her she's smokin' hot. I do want to tell her she looks pretty but can't get the words out to make it happen.

After too many pictures in the tiny living room at Randall's house, we all jump into a bunch of parent-driven minivans and smoosh into the backseat. I awkwardly make small talk with the dad driving us until we get dropped off at the high school.

The sidewalks are icy, and Claire leans into me to keep from falling as we walk toward to the building. I figure, if she can walk on those toothpicks, the least I can do is not bring up my bruised ankle, since so far it's holding up.

I open the front door and a group of kids swooshes right past Claire and into the school. We rush through the door before anyone else thinks I'm standing there as a doorman. There's a long line for the coat check, but while we wait, we attempt to talk over the throbbing beat escaping from the dance. Finally, it's our turn. We hand over our jackets, leaving our phones in the pockets.

Claire and I slip into the noisy fray and head toward the music. The other girls teeter toward the party with their dates swaggering by their sides. We follow the booming, pulsing sounds as we enter the gym. It's dark as midnight, with twinkling lights flashing all over the room. Claire makes a beeline for the bleachers, slips off her shoes, and sticks her wrist corsage in one of them. I laugh. There's a long row of flower-stuffed heels.

When she steps back over to where I'm standing, I see her toenails are painted bright pink, the same pink dotting each of her fingernails.

I'm not taking any chances tonight, so my ankle is taped up under my sock. I downed two Advil, and, luckily, I'm feeling pretty good. For the next three hours, we jump more than dance. The girls try to avoid getting their feet stepped on by the guys, which is tricky in the dark. The guys fist bump and chest bump. The room is hot as Hades, and the sweating is ridiculous.

Every few songs, Claire and I duck out to the cafeteria for a water break and then head back into the scrum. It's too loud to talk, it's uncomfortably hot, and every inch of the dance floor is spoken for.

Zuzu is across the room in a purple dress with matching purple streaks in her hair, dancing with a guy from the wrestling team. He's a huge kid named Jackson, who made it to the state finals last year, she said, and has an even better chance to clinch a title in his weight class this year. She looks over and gives me a thumbs-up.

Annie's wearing a short red dress. She comes over and leans into Claire, whispering something in her ear. Claire smiles and nods her head, and Annie moves away, waving at me as she heads back into the frenzy.

A slower dance tune fires up, "Daylight" by Maroon 5. Awkward. We decide to take a break and go sit on the bleachers to watch from the sidelines, as couples pair up and move together more closely. Then, another even slower song starts up, "Ho Hey" by the Lumineers. It is a Valentine's Dance after all. We sit that one out, too.

Finally, the DJ spins a dance tune, LMFAO's "Party Rock Anthem." We look at each other and head back toward the center of the room, where hundreds of teenagers are doing that crazy shuffling thing LMFAO does in their video. Some kids even start showing off their Gumby breakdance moves.

I'm completely exhausted after three hours of weaving in rhythm with the crowd, and my shirt is drenched with sweat. I'm having a blast, even though my ankle's feeling wobbly. I choose to worry about that tomorrow. My more immediate worry is I smell bad, but then a quick whiff of the air assures me that has to be a pretty common concern in this room.

The DJ screams out "Okay, North Plains! *Make it count!*" as he plays the last song, "Call Me Maybe." So, somehow, the jumping gets higher and the chest bumps get fiercer, and we all sing along to the lyrics. I take it down, because I don't know how much more my ankle can take, and I'm so ready when we walk out into the freezing night and load into a parent's minivan.

Some of our group goes to a kid, Roger's, house after the dance, where they've stashed beers in his basement fridge. Claire tells me she's beat and ready to head home, and I'm glad to hear it. I am completely spent and tired of pretending my ankle isn't throbbing.

Later, lying in bed, I replay the night and how purely awesome it was. My hair is wet on my pillow after a cleansing shower, and, still sticking to Eric's treatment plan, I have a bag of frozen peas draped over my ankle. I grab my phone to text Claire.

Hey.

I press send, not sure if she'll get all the meaning I packed into those three little letters at 1:30 a.m.

Hey. I had a really great time.

Yeah. Same.

I think to myself as I drift to sleep, *Hey. I have a girlfriend.*

CHAPTER THIRTY-FOUR

I wake up to the sun peeking through the bottom of the room's two blinds. The alarm clock reads almost noon.

Obeying the powerful rumbles of my stomach, I swing my feet onto the floor to head for sustenance and drop straight to the ground as a searing pain rockets up my leg. I cringe. My right ankle has blown up to twice its normal size.

"*Fuck*!" I yell out loud to nobody.

I hobble down the stairs, using the railing for support, and hop into the kitchen with my phone in hand. When I sit, I rest my ankle carefully on the nearby chair and look around for anyone who can tend to me. While three adults live in this house, nobody is rushing to my side.

I text Mom, and five minutes later she walks through the back door carrying a reusable shopping bag full of groceries in each hand.

"How was the dance?" she asks as she sets the bags on the counter and then notices my balloon of an ankle draped over the chair. "Oh, that much fun, huh?" She cracks a smile.

"Mom, this isn't funny. It hurts like hell!"

"I won't say I told you that you should have gone to see Eric one more time. Remember, you said you were feeling good."

"Mom, I'm suffering here."

Mom grabs a bag of frozen peas from the freezer then Advil from the cabinet and pours me a glass of water from the tap.

"Here you go," she says sweetly, dropping the peas in my lap and slapping the meds and water next to me on the kitchen table. "First thing tomorrow, I'll drop you off at school, and we'll see what Eric says."

After downing two painkillers, I sit like a prisoner for twenty minutes, icing my ankle, while Mom peppers me with dance questions. Hovering behind me, she looks at the pictures from last night on my phone that Claire sent plus a few group shots we took at Randall's.

At 7 a.m. sharp on Monday, I prop myself against the wall outside the training room for twenty minutes until Eric arrives, a large, black duffel bag draped over his right shoulder. He looks at me warily.

"What's going on?" he asks in a friendly tone as he unlocks the door.

"It just blew up yesterday," I say. "I don't know."

As he strides into the room, he pats a chair. I hobble over to it and sit my butt down, extending my ankle. Using my good foot, I push off my Adidas sandal so Eric can examine it.

He looks up. "Is this dance related? I have to warn you, I went to North Plains back in the day, so I know everything about this school."

"Um, yeah. It is kinda," I answer sheepishly.

After pushing down on every tender spot of my ankle and watching me repeatedly wince, he says, "Luckily, this is just a minor setback. Your ankle will be better in a few weeks, but you're going to want to take it easy. I'd say no gym class or basketball for at least six weeks. We'll add in a few sessions of ultrasound to reduce the swelling, but, otherwise, just follow the same protocol as before. But take it more seriously this time."

I nod in agreement.

He adds, "Have a parent contact the school nurse to okay the ultrasound. Then, come by during lunch or after school, and we can get started."

I text Eric's instructions to Mom as I limp out the door. A half hour later, she texts me back.

All done.

I spend my lunch period in the training room. Eric spreads a cold, clear gel on my foot and then runs a wand over every inch of my ankle for ten minutes.

After sitting there in silence, I wonder if he may know my mom. Wouldn't that be freaky?

"My mom went to school here, too," I tell him. "Stephanie Santi."

"Really? Steph Santi is your mom?" He looks up at me, surprised. "Wow. You knew her?"

"Well, I knew *of* her. Everybody in high school probably did. She's a year older than me. She was homecoming queen her senior year—I remember that."

"Yeah, I know." Grandma showed me those pictures one day.

"I was a high school All-American here. Baseball. I tore my ACL skiing over winter break senior year. Spent my final high school season sitting on the bench. It was torture not being able to play with my teammates."

What a bummer that must have been. "Is that how you got into this?" I ask, genuinely interested.

"Yes. I spent six months in rehab after my surgery and really connected with how the therapists got me basically back to normal."

He puts the wand away and motions we're done with the session. As I limp out the door, he adds, "Roman, I got better because I worked at it really hard. If you want to play basketball again, you have to do the same. I'll see you here same time Wednesday."

I like this guy. He knows his stuff, and he's made me see the light.

During the week, I visit Eric a few more times for ultrasound treatments and keep up my part of the bargain. It sucks that I'm benched for six weeks, but I get that I have to give my ankle time to completely heal. After that, Eric says, I should be 100 percent.

I'm itching to get back to basketball.

CHAPTER THIRTY-FIVE

There is an honor code in Spoken Word: Respect the mic. I've listened to a lot of students share their most intimate stories. I've witnessed the hugging and sometimes the tears every time students recite poems that lay bare their darkest demons and emotions. I haven't been on the giving or receiving end of these post-mic hug/cry fests quite yet. But now I'm so deep into this Spoken Word world, I cannot avoid the group hugs.

I've written a lot of poems, some good but most pretty bad. I've tiptoed around the edges of my own issues. I feel protective of my story—it's mine and I haven't been ready to share or cry over it. I haven't let my guard down enough to let the group in on something that defines me so completely but that I hide so damn well, I can sometimes forget it's even there.

What is "it" you ask?

I'll tell you. Loss.

I have never met my father. My mom may not get why that matters so much, since I have her and my grandparents and so much more. Which I do. But still, it does *matter*.

When I was old enough to ask the questions I wanted answers to, I lived like a prince in a palace. I had everything I could want: a warm bed, a big house, family, great friends. I had a father-type figure who was larger than life. I'll always have this mom who's loving and carefree. But somewhere in my head—maybe it popped up from my heart, to be honest—I knew that was not the whole truth.

Sure, I had a lot of things. I had a lot of people who really cared about me. But there is a dad out there I don't know and who does not know about me. All the glamour and glitz of living large in L.A. couldn't make that less true. Less important.

Still, I didn't feel I had the right to complain. To ask for more when I obviously had so much. I can see now I also didn't want to hurt Kirk's feelings or shine a spotlight on a decision my mom made when she was twenty years old and believed she knew what was best.

And that is what Spoken Word is teaching me: to allow these feelings to the surface. To be more honest with myself about what matters to me. I realize now it's more than okay to speak my truth about what's been bottled up for too long. I see how it helps to bare our souls, first on paper and then in front of a group of people who will hear and support us unconditionally.

While I was surrounded by so much comfort and security at Kirk's, I didn't have a clue there would be so many fucked-up paths out there that were leading so many kids to live in messed-up situations. I didn't know some of my classmates were walking around feeling intensely misunderstood, fearful, and stressed. So, even though I sleep on a lumpy pullout sofa bed in my grandparents' home, with a dad somewhere in the world who doesn't know I exist, I count myself lucky. It could be so much worse.

Learning about club members' raw reality just makes us feel so knitted together. Whether it's a big hurt or a little one or just a perceived one, nobody judges, nobody gossips. We share our stories. We respect the mic.

For example, club member Christian Thurman speaks the full honest truth with the poem he recites in front of our group:

> *Freshman year I took acid before school*
> *The windows in my brain's dorm room suddenly flew*
> *open*
> *Everything inside began to sway*
> *left to right caught like a branch in an obliterating*
> *tornado*
> *I shouldn't be twitching this fast*
> *I feel like snapping.*
> *My pupils turn rainbow*

I feel like I am trying
To solve a Rubik's Cube
the squares are made of reality and fantasy
The school's walls turned into the bars of a gray
    penitentiary
Even feathers became scary, turning into hairy
    wildebeests
I just wanted to see normal
The day passes slow as a molasses stuck in lake shore
    drive traffic
Finally, at 5:00 PM the trip ended
I promised myself never to fall back on spinning
    rainbows.

And then Chelsea Bonner stands and announces her poem's title, "Taking Anxiety as a Lover." In it, she puts words to an emotion I, too, have wrestled with since I had to put L.A. in the rearview mirror.

Long ago, I let it rinse through me and
Sink in shallows too deep to reach by mere hands.
I carved body into question mark and let you in.
You've made a garment of me.
An animated sleeve I no longer recognize.

Anxiety, you are the perfect lover.
The one I curl into at night.
I line my shelves with your books as if
One day they'll offer an answer, but
They are light and leafless.
I once considered washing you down into oblivion.
Made a net of hands to fall forward without you.
But I do not wish to dull your senses.
Instead I wish, in silence, that one day

I will garner courage to stand up to you
When you are wrong.

Okay, heavy stuff. I know.

Luckily, life can be full of awesome moments. It's those everyday realities we also want to dissect. Sometimes, we want to write about sitting on the bleachers at a baseball game, going on vacation, and Thanksgiving at Grandma's. Or explore universal truths like complicated friendships or failed relationships.

Here's one I like, by Zoë Amundson, that doesn't bum me out:

My eyes swallow sun on summer days.
Smoothing my hand along the city's lining.
Ben shows his neck to the sky
and traces my palms' grooves.
For the last time our skin is untouched
marked.
He says, "summer's gonna last forever"
and holds the clock,
binds the time until his hands get tired,
and September calls for us.
It's these summer days that restore our souls and
*   furnish our*
hearts.
We are the young,
allowing ourselves to sink.
Just enough to escape drowning.

So, there's that. I think it reminds me of L.A. I mean, that was the last time I had sun and summer. Well, actually, every day out there was sun and summer, really. Probably that's why I picked this poem to share with you all. And between us, liking Claire has made me a bit soft.

The real scoop is that lots of us have built up angst and a message we want to put out that the world may not be so ready to hear. Well, tough shit! Message sent.

CHAPTER THIRTY-SIX

I'm at the kitchen table, doing what I do best: eating. I'm taking a well-deserved study break. I have a ten-page lab report on genetic coding due tomorrow, and I'm maybe halfway there.

That's when the doorbell rings.

"Roman, it's Zuzu!" Grandpa yells from the front entryway.

Zuzu walks over to the table and plops down noisily in the chair next to mine. "Hey, Roman. Your life is about to get more interesting." She grabs a handful of tortilla chips from the open bag. "I have a surprise for you."

"I'll pass," I say. "I've had enough that's interesting, don't you think?"

"How come you weren't at Spoken Word today?"

"Lab report. It's due tomorrow."

"Oh. Yeah. Those suck. Well, Mr. Collins said we're having a competition. It's next month. Eight students could win."

"I'll support you totally. You should do it."

"No, stupid. It's for *you*. The winners get to go to England in June to perform in a poetry showcase run by Mr. Collins's friend." She stops talking to chomp on a chip.

I look at her, confused. "Yeah, great. You should go then."

"*Roman!* Has that lab report sucked all the brains out of you? You should go. England… You know, hello? It's near France."

"Oh." My wheels start turning. "Yes, that's kind of a big deal then, isn't it?"

Zuzu nods and smiles. "The winners need to help raise the money for airfare and stuff, which he says is doable."

"That would be pretty crazy." The possibilities run through my head.

"Roman, let's get you to England. Do I have permission to do that Facebook stalk thing we talked about the first day we met?"

"Wow, Zuzu, you are such a schemer. I never talked about that. You did. I probably wouldn't even make the cut."

"You would, though. That poem you read to Claire was awesome."

"But what if he, like, doesn't want to know me? What if I do all this work, and then Marcel is, like, 'no thanks'?" Of course, that is my greatest fear. The biggest reason I haven't pushed Mom on this before. Because what if he doesn't care?

"Roman, seriously?! Let's just think about what if he *does* care! I mean he's your father!"

"But—" Zuzu shakes her head at my downer attitude. Maybe she's right. "You mean who wouldn't want a wonderful son like me to contact him out of the blue?" I say, half-joking.

She grins like I'm half-funny.

Grandpa walks in to offer Zuzu a ride home on his way to teaching his night class.

After she leaves, I sit at the kitchen table a long time, thinking about what she's just shared with me. I find it completely impossible to focus on my lab report when thoughts of my father are now in my head.

I dive into analyzing strips of DNA, hoping the pure agony of this assignment I've left to the last minute will distract me from the bomb Zuzu just dropped in the room that has left my current reality completely unrecognizable. She's given me the best reason I've ever had to try and find my father.

Which would also mean confronting my mom about, well, finding my dad.

"Hi, Roman honey," Grandma says as she walks into the kitchen. "Do you want me to see if Grandpa can help you with your lab report when he gets home tonight? I know he says he wants you to learn it yourself, but I'm sure he wants to see you get it right."

"Thanks, Grandma, but it's on a specific activity we did. I have to analyze the findings and then show the results. It's just boring is all."

"You've got a lot going on, it sounds like. I'll leave you to it." She ruffles my hair and walks away.

If she only knew. I kinda wish I could discuss this bombshell of trying to go to England and maybe meeting my dad with my grandparents.

Does Zuzu's idea make sense? Should I open up this can of worms after it's been sealed so tight all my life?

I think it does. I think I should.

But I don't want to gamble on the possibility that talking about this opportunity could actually shut it down. I don't want to hear, "It's not a good idea" from my practical grandpa, or "We need to consider all the angles first" from my philosophical grandma.

I pull out my phone and text Zuzu.

I'll enter. Will you?

I press send. She texts right back.

OK. Let's both go for it!

You have to promise. This is between us. Nobody else can know.

Nobody? Not even Claire?

This is 100% private.

I totally get it. My lips are sealed.

If somehow the London thing happens THEN you have my permission to stalk away.

Operation Marcel begins.

I reply with an emoji because, honestly, I am speechless.

There's only one thing to do. I've got to come up with a Spoken Word poem that's beyond amazing.

CHAPTER THIRTY-SEVEN

Spoken Word Club. Tuesday.

I sit with Claire, Zuzu, and Annie, and I brought Randall with me for dude support. He covers the tennis and volleyball teams for the school newspaper, so I mentioned Spoken Word club to him at lunch last week and told him about the London competition. I also put in a few words about the low guy-to-girl ratio. He was interested after that, especially since he and Lauren, his date for the Valentine's Dance, are "just friends."

"Good afternoon," Mr. Collins begins. He stands up in front of the room, like usual, but there a number of new faces in the audience. This competition is looking tougher all the time. "As many of you know, our school has received an exciting opportunity. A few years ago, a group of students from England came over to our Louder Than a Bomb competition with their teacher, Bill Taylor. Well, now Mr. Taylor is inviting our students to be guest performers at their Roundhouse Poetry Slam in London, which will take place on June 14."

Peter's hand shoots up. "But isn't that after school is done?"

"Yes. Here, we will be already starting summer vacation. Over in England, they structure the school year a bit differently. But also—there's a but—because our seniors will have graduated and will no longer be students of the high school at that time, I'm afraid the competition will be open only to all our current freshman through junior students," Mr. Collins explains. Peter nods.

Gina—she's a senior—yells out, "*Seriously?* That sucks!"

Mr. Collins acknowledges Gina's frustration with a frown and a nod in her direction then picks up a stack of flyers from the desk and hands them to Max in the first row to pass around.

"On April 10, that's just about a month away, we're going to hold our competition in this room. Eight of you will be chosen to go to England. The details are on this flyer. Attached is a commitment sheet. that must be signed by each participant and a parent or guardian then handed in to me by the deadline listed here before you can enter the competition. The same rules apply. Every poem must be two minutes or less, be a new poem we haven't heard, and can be about any topic as long as it is appropriate for school."

Annie raises her hand. "Who's judging the contest?" she asks when called on.

"I'm excited about this part as well," Mr. Collins says. "I will be a judge, of course. And there will be four Spoken Word alumni who will help judge. We'll follow the same ten-point scale we use for Louder Than a Bomb. After talking about this opportunity, we decided we want to add a special element, to make it a bit different than the way we score Louder Than a Bomb. We're going to have ten percent of the vote be from the audience."

"Kinda like *Dancing with the Stars*," Gina says.

"Sure. Kinda like that." Mr. Collins grins. "We'll have a ballot with each student participant's name listed and everyone in our audience will be allowed to vote for three performers and then turn in their ballot as they leave."

Students start to snap their fingers in unison. That's another Spoken Word quirk students display after they like a comment made or when some striking line stands out in a poem. It also substitutes for clapping after a student finishes reciting a piece. Some days, there's lots of snapping.

A student I don't know hands me a few flyers. I take one and pass the rest to Claire, who is sitting next to me. Randall passes the flyers to the person next to him without taking one then looks at me and shakes his head. It didn't take him long to learn that Spoken Word is not his thing.

My flyer says:

London Teen Poetry Slam

North Plains Team Selection — Thursday April 10 at 3:20
p.m. Room 330

<u>*The criteria will include:*</u> *writing talent (original, meaningful), talent as a performer/stage presence, dependability/reliability, ability to be a supportive teammate, leadership qualities, charisma, positive attitude, strong work ethic, dedication to SW Club, ability to respond to constructive criticism, risk-taking ability, and the impact that making the team would have on the individual. School grades will also be a deciding factor if you can participate.*

If you want to be considered for the Slam team, you MUST attend/perform on this TRY-OUT date!

After a few minutes of quiet, Mr. Collins reads a section of the flyer. "Each team member will be expected to write, revise, memorize, and rehearse their individual poem, as well as contribute to the creation and performance of a group piece. Team members will be expected to be supportive toward and helpful with each other. Any questions?" His eyes skim all the faces staring eagerly in his direction.

It's amazing, but nobody has one. I read on to the bottom of the page:

Student Commitment:

In order to be a team member, one has to commit to making the North Plains Slam Team his/her number one extracurricular activity. In other words, our meetings/rehearsals must take precedence over other **clubs** *(i.e., Gospel Choir, or Dance Club),* **teams** *(i.e., baseball),* **activities**, *and* **jobs**. *One must clear this with other sponsors, coaches, supervisors, etc. in advance.*

I don't have those commitments going on now. Sure, I'm getting back into basketball pick-up games here and there, now that my ankle feels great, but there is nothing getting in the way of me doing this.

Here's my challenge. Can I write a mind-blowing poem for the competition that doesn't delve into my emotional trauma about my dad? Or should I try to kick these feelings around, something I have never allowed myself to do?

What can I write about that will get the judges to go WOW? To pick me? What can I say out loud in front of these judges I've never met that is so damn good, it gets me to England?

CHAPTER THIRTY-EIGHT

Sitting at the desk in my room after dinner, I pull the permission slip out of my backpack and reread it. Is Mom even going to sign this damn thing? Is my plan all for nothing? I text her.

Mom, can you come in my room? I want to ask you a ?

She hates how I text her when we are both in the house. But sometimes it just has to be done. I'm so used to texting her anyway, since she's been in L.A. so much, and I never know when she's heading back there next. I have to work this out ASAP.

Really, Roman?

Then, a few minutes later, she's there, sitting on the edge of the chair in front of my desk, watching me pace back and forth like a caged animal.

"Roman, you're scaring me. What's the matter?"

I drop onto my bed and face her square on. I hand over the permission slip.

She reads it over slowly. "Okay. Sure, Roman. This sounds thrilling." She reaches for a pen on my desk.

"Mom, if I get chosen, I want to ask Marcel to be there. To see me perform. I—"

"Oh. No. That's not possible. This is not possible." She pulls her hand away like the paper's caught on fire. "I can't sign this if that is what you want. Roman, it can't happen."

I sit up straight, shaking, as I gather my thoughts. "Mom, I'm not really asking you. I want to know my father. You can't keep me from him forever."

"I'm not sure if I can help you," she says, bristling, then picks up the permission slip and stands. "I will think about this. But there are so many ways it could go wrong. I just want to protect you from what sounds like a really bad idea."

She storms out, slamming the door behind her, before I can get another word in.

Is this a bad idea? Or just a crazy one?

I realize this could all blow up in my face. But I also know, if there is anything in the world worth me taking a chance on, this is it.

CHAPTER THIRTY-NINE

The next morning, Mom and I tiptoe around each other as I get myself out the door to school. My grandparents stay out of the way, too—smart!—as the house is on edge. I invite myself to Randall's after school, and when his mom asks if I would like to stay for dinner, I don't hesitate in saying yes. After Randall's dad drops me home, I prepare myself for more steely silence around Mom.

"Hi, Grandma," I say with false cheerfulness as I head past the kitchen sink where she is washing a coffee mug.

"Roman, how was your day?" she asks, returning my bouquet of cheer.

"It was a day," I answer and head up the stairs toward my room. As I open the door, I almost step on a piece of paper on the floor—the permission slip! On top of it, written on a yellow Post-it:

> *If this is the journey you wish to take, I will not stand in your way.*
>
> *Love you, Mom*

She has signed the permission slip.

I should be happy about this. I get it. But I don't need Mom giving me half of what I need from her. Her standing aside could mean a lot of things.

Obviously, writing an amazing poem isn't the only thing I need to worry about. There's Mom. To her, Marcel is the past. To me, he's my past but also my present and my future. Will she even help me find him, if I win a spot on the team?

CHAPTER FORTY

March 16 is Zuzu's sixteenth birthday. She thinks there is a word for that, when your birthdate is the same as your age. We Google it on our phones while we walk into town and, after a bunch of dead links, learn it's called a golden birthday. I realize my grandpa would have known the answer to that—I should have just texted him and saved a bunch of data. He's like a walking Wikipedia.

Today, Zuzu has green streaks in her hair in honor of St. Patrick's Day. She wanted to go for a Shamrock Shake at McDonald's, but since I'm buying, I overruled that idea.

Instead, I'm treating her to a birthday milkshake at Potbelly's. Mother Nature has actually given us a sunny, warmish day so a freezing-cold Oreo milkshake is the exact perfect thing for a post-lunch snack.

I hope you've had a Potbelly milkshake at least once, because they are sooo good. Not as good as Portillo's, but then nothing in the world beats a cake shake. No contest. Game over.

"Bad news," Zuzu says as we walk down Lake Street. "I'm not going to enter the competition for London."

"*No way!*" I scream, stopping in my tracks. "We're doing that together I thought!"

"I know. But I showed the flyer to my mom. She says that's when we're making our annual pilgrimage to Disney World. My dad already has the time off, and the hotel's booked."

"Well, that sucks!" I have to readjust my image. I pictured Zuzu making the cut. I really did.

"You've been to Disney like a million times—can't you miss it?" I ask.

She looks at me, like, *Really? Are you crazy?*

"You know my family. This is number-one importante. I'm totally bummed. But I'm gonna root for you to win this thing. I wanna help rally the troops."

"Well, Claire may not enter, either," I say. "Her dad has signed her up for some field hockey camp at Notre Dame. He already paid for it and really wants her to do it."

"Oh, field hockey or England?" Zuzu balances her palms in the air like scales. The England hand stays up higher, like it really isn't an equal choice. England is so much better.

"She may enter anyway, and if she has the choice, then she'll try to figure it out. But she's totally confused about it," I add.

I hold open the door to Potbelly's and head to the counter to order our shakes. I convince Zuzu to try the Oreo shake. She usually gets boring vanilla. Some bearded guy plays acoustic guitar in a corner of the restaurant next to an open guitar case. I throw the meager quarter and dime I get back from the cashier on top of the other change and few dollars inside, and then we sit in a nearby booth with our shakes.

"Wow. This is good," Zuzu says after her first sip. "I used to think you were the most food-obsessed guy. Then I met Jackson. He's totally got you beat. But in a scary way."

"Scary food-obsessed? How's that?" I am genuinely intrigued.

"Well, you know, he's a wrestler, so it's all about making weight. One day, he'll eat every carb in sight, and then the next day eat like yogurt and carrot sticks. And some days, he doesn't even eat at all!"

"No way could I do that. Not eat at all." Even the thought of it scares me.

"Oh, but you could eat yogurt and carrots sticks?"

I shake away that thought quickly. "That's not happening either."

We sit and talk long after we've drained our milkshakes. Zuzu finishes hers first, so I think I've converted her from vanilla. After a while, one of her friends walks in with her dad and makes a beeline over to our table, another thing so different here, in the suburbs. In L.A., very rarely would I be out at a restaurant or store and run into someone I know. But here, it happens all the time.

Zuzu introduces me to Emily, and the three of us talk while her dad goes to the counter to order. She's a sophomore like Zuzu and wears a soccer uniform with grass stains all over her knees and soccer socks. Soccer still conjures up bad memories for me. I try to keep my mind focused on the conversation, but it wanders back to L.A. I wonder if soccer is ruined for me forever because of Mom and Joel and that lame movie.

While we talk, Emily's phone buzzes.

"Ha! My dad is asking me what I want to eat." She laughs at the screen and then texts her food order to a phone just twenty feet away.

After Emily and her dad grab their food to go, we head back to my house. My grandma wants to wish Zuzu a happy birthday and even bought her a present—some dream catcher thing to put over her bed.

"So, I never asked you," Zuzu says. "What was your deal with girls before you came here? Did you have girlfriends?"

"I hung out with my guy friends mostly," I answer. I really didn't have a friend who was a girl before I met Zuzu.

"So, Claire's, like, your first girlfriend?"

"She's different than the girls I knew in L.A.," I say then decide to change the topic. "I'm bummed about you not doing the competition."

"It's fine. Really. But I'm going to get a cheering section together for you!"

"Don't embarrass me, Zuz. Promise?"

"Too late. That's what I'm planning. A cheering section. Get ready."

"Can't wait," I say, as we turn the corner and head down the block toward my home.

CHAPTER FORTY-ONE

Sitting on my bed, propped up against a pillow that shields me from the hard, white wall, I scrawl some sentences in my gray notebook and then read them over.

> *I had it down cold*
> *Living life like a king*
> *Along for a ride in a mansion*
> *More than I could ever dream*
> *Crashing down*
> *Because mom's messes become mine*

I realize this is too honest. Too transparent. I dig deeper still. Reading my next attempt through, it's a miss. I try again. Again. And again.

I tell myself I can't give up until I write a dope poem. I close myself in my room after dinner every night and fill my gray notebook with too many words that end up beneath slashes and scratches.

My writing cuts in so many directions. I feel I'm getting further away from what I want to say. Finally, after many attempts, I find my voice. The words start to spill out all at once. That's when I step up my game and keep working it. Sure, some of it's made up, but nobody has to know that. It's my truth; I didn't say it was *the* truth.

Now I've got a poem I'm calling "Falling into Place." I'm blown away by what I wrote. Not because it's so amazing. Because, in this

Spoken Word poem, I'm expressing a part of me I thought I would never talk about. And I'm saying it in a way that only I understand the true meaning.

CHAPTER FORTY-TWO

I guess I should have grabbed an umbrella before I walked Ozzie. Now, my jeans are soaked through. I also should have done something about *that* before I sat my butt down at my desk five minutes ago to start writing a paper for Mr. Katz's English class on "Satire in the *Adventures of Huckleberry Finn*."

I've marked the "ironic" parts of the book, and now it's time to pull my thoughts together, so I can give Mr. Katz what he wants. Then, hopefully, I can get what I want… An A.

My brain hurts just thinking about the hours that lie in front of me with this paper. But it isn't going to write itself.

There's a knock on my partly open bedroom door, and before I even turn my head, Mom walks in and sits on my bed.

"Hey, Mom, what's up?" I swivel to face her. I've been on my best behavior since we came to a truce over Marcel.

"Well, the school's trainer, Eric, Facebook messaged me. He wants you to come by this week so he can check out your ankle strength."

"Yeah, sure. I can do that one day at lunch."

"Okay. And, well, he also asked me to go out to dinner with him this weekend in Chicago."

I knew it! That Facebook message thing about my ankle seemed weird the minute Mom said it. *Smooth, Eric.*

"Mom, I don't care if you do that," I say truthfully.

Actually, it would be good for her to get out more. The only thing she's doing is getting up really early to help some lady named Irene slap makeup on TV news anchors. Oh, and of course her almost daily pilgrimages to some hot yoga place she's obsessed with.

And then there's Grandpa trying to get her to take up jogging. He even made sure she went to see his buddy Danny at Fleet Feet, to be fitted for running shoes. Mom has gone jogging a few times, but she tells me she's terrible at it and can barely run a mile. Running is not my thing, either, so I feel her pain.

"You see, Roman, I don't want to do anything to make you mad or mess up. I just don't trust my judgment these days. I asked Grandma, and she says I should go. But Traci says, because he works at the school, maybe it's not a good idea."

"Mom, if you want to, just go. He's not my teacher or anything."

"Okay. I will then. We have some mutual friends, so it would be fun to hear what people have been up to."

"Cool." Then I take this opening to ask her for a favor. "Mom, can I have some money? Claire and I are going out to dinner Saturday night. She says we can eat anywhere but Chipotle. Or Five Guys. I think that means she wants to go someplace nice."

"Looks that way, hon," she says sweetly. Just as I've tried to play the good son part to a T, she's been doing her best, these past few days, to show she's firmly in my corner. "I know I haven't been giving you an allowance here. I'd be happy to treat you two, so you can go out somewhere with a waiter."

"Thanks, Mom," I mumble as she walks out.

I can't tell her the real reason for this date. Claire and I got in a huge fight after school yesterday. She says I spend too much time with Zuzu. She even asked if I "like" like Zuzu.

Zuzu and I are totally just friends, I told her. That's the truth. I did like her for a hot minute when we first met. Of course, I wouldn't tell Claire that. But now, well, no. We're buds.

I'm really into Claire. I guess I have to show her that. It's just hard to hang out when, every day at 5:30 p.m., she has lacrosse team practice or games.

I know Claire says no Chipotle, but I wonder if that means no Mexican food… I'm thinking we should go to Maya. They have killer guac and chips. And waiters.

CHAPTER FORTY-THREE

What: The Competition
When: Thursday after school
Where: Room 330. Packed house.
27 kids.
(I go 14th)
Friday is when winners will be announced.

We're in the room where Spoken Word club meets. The same stage I stood on when I asked Claire to go to the dance. The same stage I've performed on probably seven times.

Mr. Collins divides the twenty-seven of us into three groups of nine. I sit in the front row with my eight other competitors. Joey, sitting next to me, intently reads over his poem on his phone in a last-minute case of nerves.

The first group of nine stands on the stage in a sort of crooked line. When it's time to perform, the next student takes a few steps to center stage. There is no mic today, even though kids sit ten rows deep.

Mr. Collins, wearing a yellow, red, and blue plaid shirt, walks to center stage and fires up the competition. That's how he starts everything. He says something cool that totally kicks my competitive butt into gear. Today, he's on his game.

Looking out at the faces in the room, he welcomes us and then gets the ball rolling. "Mr. Taylor just told me some great news I want to share right away. He has secured a grant from the British Council that will help offset some of the hotel costs for our group." The room fills with the sound of fingers snapping. "Remember," he adds, his voice rising to ricochet around the room. "What started on the page ends on this stage!"

He turns to smile at the nine students behind him, who shuffle nervously in place, and then pivots to face the front of the room again.

"For everyone here, just remember to be in the moment with your poems. For those of us in the audience, let's make sure we're supportive and just enjoy hearing each other's words. When you hear a striking line, what can you do?"

A bunch of students start to snap.

"Right." He pauses. "Immediately after school on Friday, I will post a list of the eight student winners on my office door." He then sweeps his hands to the back row, where the judges are sitting, and explains they are alumni and past Spoken Word competitors. Then he asks them to say a bit about themselves.

The alumni judges stand up. It's comical how different they look one from the other. The first judge, who introduces himself as Justin, is a bald, African-American guy with dorky glasses who wears a black-and-white polka dot bow tie and black suit jacket. Next to him is another African-American guy, Darryl, who wears a blue Nike-swoosh sweatshirt and has short hair spiked up straight. The third judge, Brandon, is one of the tallest and skinniest white guys I've ever seen; he totally belongs on the court. Then there's a kinda big girl, Patti, with short, dark hair, wearing black leggings and a T-shirt that says "Love Yourself First."

After the introductions, Mr. Collins continues. "So, now we are about to start. I want all the performers to speak loudly and begin with their name and the name of their poem. Everyone in the audience should have a piece of paper with all the competitors' names on it. You each can vote for your top three favorite Spoken Word poets at the end. Hand the ballots to our English Division chairperson, Ms. Alton, as you walk out the door, please."

Ms. Alton stands up and gives a quick wave. "Good luck to all our competitors," she says before sitting back down.

Mr. Collins looks around the room. "Now audience, remember, when you vote, this is not a popularity contest. I want you to put your support behind who you think would best represent our school in

London." Finally, he adds, "Okay, audience and slam performers, let's do this."

He steps off the stage, leaving the first nine students to make their mark. I won't bore you with all the details... Some do great, some do good, and some not so good.

Next, it's our group's turn. The nine of us shuffle to the stage and stand next to each other, facing the crowd.

First up is a junior, T.J., who always puts on a show, and today doesn't disappoint. He stands at the front of the room in jeans and an unzipped black sweatshirt over a Beck concert T-shirt, with his signature bright-blue Beats headphones hanging around his neck.

Zuzu says all her friends are crazy for T.J., though she swears he's not her "type." He's a guitar player who writes his own songs, a few he's put on YouTube, but in school, he's known as a man of few words. His hair is this shining mass of yellow exactly the color of gold. He loves to write poems that are depressing and full of angst.

He starts out with:

> *When there's no place to GO*
> *Where do you go?*
> *I just want my own room.*
> *That's not much to ask for.*
> *My own private space in the world.*
> *To practice my music, to think,*
> *To write. To just be ME.*
> *I don't need silk sheets,*
> *though it would be nice...*

Everyone knows his dad is an Oak Park cop. Still, T.J. doesn't filter his poems one bit. I guess he's rocking an irresistible combination of coolness and chill. He finishes his poem:

...And one day when I am no longer a kid
living under your thumb
I will spend my waking moments
conquering mountains
and swimming with sharks
and my nights eating filet mignon in a king-size bed
with silk sheets.

The room explodes with snapping as he takes a step back into line.

Next comes Hannah's poem about her father's smoking, his yellow teeth, and a smell that "sticks in the air no matter how many windows are open."

Joey holds his phone in his hand as he looks out at the audience and recites its name, "Young and Proud." He then breaks into a rhythmic rap about being too old for a lollipop at the dentist and how he reads comic books, but never graphic novels, for fun. He does look down at the screen a few times when he falters but then gets right back into the moment. In the end, his poem is funny and light, but I'm not sure how that plays with the judges.

Then there's a real honest poem about depression by a girl, Carissa, who wears a denim jacket. She says it is called, "Bad Penny," and then speaks clearly and strongly. More than one of her lines has me snapping. Like: "after losing myself among strangers as a freshman in this huge scary place and finding myself again among friends, I know I am not a product of the world but of myself."

Olivia, a shy girl who goes before me, holds a piece of paper in front of her as she looks down and reads her poem with shaky hands. It's about her brother's many bad asthma attacks and calling 911 and ambulances racing to the door. She rushes through it, taking few breaths between words, so the sentences run together. That makes it hard to focus on what's being said.

Then I'm up. I stand alone in front of my classmates and look out at friendly faces. Claire, whose field hockey camp won out, with Zuzu sitting next to her and Randall.

I do the best I can to bring my words to life. I know this is not for fun, not today. Today, it's a serious competition of words. I fire up my voice to bring it:

I am Son Grandson Friend Student
Awesome Baller
Still, there was a mask I wore
for your benefit
to deny a part of me.
Looming in the distance
a sign. Huge Red Letters
They read KEEP OUT!
DANGER AHEAD!
Guarded by a big scary beast
that I've known since childhood.
I played by your rules and stayed away.
Until I couldn't.
And then day after day I would inch closer
beyond ready to drop the false face
Until I finally burst in where I was told not to go.
How stupid I felt
there was no monster after all
only reflection bouncing off light.
My shadow. Looming.
Because what we don't know is
always larger than life.
Now there's another sign
Flashing Green Letters
pointing still further
toward my destiny.
I take one huge step
forward

SOIT BRAVE, it says
Be Brave
and that I am.
So, I walk straight through
I abandon my mask
squint into the bright sun
to discover YOU
and my whole self.

I've done it! I got through it all without missing a beat. I've said my piece. My peace.

The guy after me, Desmond, recites his poem called "Chicago" using every part of his body—his fingers and arms flying, feet shuffling, mouth booming like he owns the room. It doesn't hurt that just his presence fills the stage. Desmond is, like, linebacker big. When he's done, Annie whispers to me that he won some "Spirit of the Slam Award" last year. I can totally see why.

The next person to take center stage is Jackie, who has got to be the goofiest dresser in the history of clothes. Seriously. Today, she's wearing black Converse Chuck Taylors that lace up to her knees, a black mesh T-shirt over a neon tank top, and ripped-up jean shorts over black tights. Enough said. Standing in front of the room, Jackie tells us her poem is called "My Journey."

I am fire orange
Full of humor, curiosity
Wanting adventure to take me places
Where only the very brave dare to go
I am clear sky turquoise blue
Cautious, uncool
Watching every step for danger
Staying on the path, eyes forward
I am foamy sea-green
Clever, confident
Courageous and bold as a drum beat

Wading off-trail through the tall grass
These colors glow brilliant and powerful
So, even when days are dark and stormy
I am guided by what sparks inside me

I have no idea what her poem means. I think Mr. Collins would say it has too many adjectives. Too much telling. He's always reminding us to zoom in on a moment, to avoid being vague, so I think she's messed that up. One thing I'll admit, she took right out of Mr. Collins's playbook his instruction to focus on something *big* and make it her own.

The audience finds a point toward the end to snap their approval, so maybe because I'm so busy being freaked out by her outfit, I'm missing something.

Annie has the final poem of the group. Her braids trail over both her shoulders, and she wears a black skirt with what Claire told me is her lucky shirt, because she wore it when she performed at Louder than a Bomb. It's a white T-shirt that reads, in fancy, black script, "Make Every Day Saturday." (That's a great idea!)

"My poem is called 'Walk This Way,'" Annie announces. Like all of us, she stands under the harsh, bright lights in front of the dingy, gray, concrete block walls. But that all softens as her words follow a steady rhythm so it feels like she's singing a song, not performing poetry.

Her face lights up as she pours her guts onto the stage, her strong voice leading us on a welcome journey. At times, she punctuates a word with her hand, gesturing in sync with the sound.

Come walk the dog with me
My dad insists
The very moment I wake up
on a Saturday morning.
It's the last thing I want to do
because Saturdays are for sleeping LATE.

Then eating
Honey Nut Cheerios in my pj's
in front of some mindless show I find on TV.
He will not take NO for an answer.
I complain, refuse, and
beat my fists on my pillow.
Nothing sways him.
Once I am on these walks,
even if we're walking in the rain,
or bundled up and trudging through
the snow, the freezing cold,
I find them pleasant
The way my dad and I joke
Joke about my fat, adorable
lazy dog
about softball
and balls that bounce off my glove,
or miss it completely
and especially about each other!
So many inside jokes and laughs.
No secrets between us.
One day, I am going to miss
these walks I so dread.

Annie kills it. Her poems always make me think. *No secrets between us.* One day that will be me and *my* dad.

We spend more than an hour sitting on hard chairs in a stuffy room being bombarded with raw, intense emotions. Mr. Collins signals to the nine of us on stage to end with a group hug, which is awkward, since we don't all know who's who. But this is how Spoken Word rolls, so I allow myself to be smushed in the circle.

CHAPTER FORTY-FOUR

There's only one other freshman guy who entered the competition, though I wasn't sure if he was really a part of Spoken Word before this. There's nothing wrong with that; a bunch of kids entered the competition whom I'd never seen before. But Max, I had noticed.

There is something about him that has me scan every club meeting for his presence. He attends most of the meetings but is always super-quiet. I feel kinda sorry for him. He's seriously beanpole-skinny. Not short or tall, hair not black or blond but closer to brown, bad case of acne. Never recited a poem, just sat alone, always seemed to be taking notes. Then, he recites this poem for the competition that, well, is probably one of the sadder things I've ever heard.

His younger brother, Robert, has leukemia, so his poem was about his mom not really being around much, because she's always in hospitals and going to doctor visits for her son. It's serious stuff. I know everyone has problems, but some people's problems are on another level completely, and that's Max. The good news is his brother is doing better—he's in remission. Robert was even in the audience when Max read his poem, and that was intense.

The day after the competition, I walk into the lunch room and find Max sitting by himself, so I take my burger over to sit by him.

He and I strategize about how it could go when Mr. Collins posts the list later today. Our conclusion: it could go any which way. There were so many good Spoken Word performers up there reciting really impressive poems.

Stay tuned.

CHAPTER FORTY-FIVE

Sitting in algebra, I watch the clock over the white board on the classroom wall strike 3:04. The end-of-the-day bell rings loudly, echoing throughout the school.

Quickly, I gather up my notebook and shoot out the door ahead of my classmates. I weave through the chaos of bodies streaming through the hallway and run up the staircase and then down the corridor to the Spoken Word office. A crush of students stands in front of the closed door as I smush myself into the back of the huddle to get a glimpse at the list taped onto the glass. A kid jumps into the tight circle behind me and tries to read the names, pushing me deeper into the group crowded around the office door.

"Dammit, man, watch it!" A girl in front of me turns around and glares at me.

"Sorry," I say, shifting slightly to the side. A few kids in front of me slide away from the door, so I move up to get a closer look at the list. I see a blur of names. One stands out.

Roman Santi

I stare a while longer to make sure I'm seeing it right. Then I step away and stand just outside the muddle of students who are intent on seeing who was chosen for London. I don't take in any other names on the list. But I am there. *Me*.

I feel not excited or scared but really just weirded out. My mind churns at the reality that I am doing this thing that's crazy and public and different, and I'm going to be doing it in London. And then there's Marcel. All of a sudden, there's no denying what I need to do now.

After a short while, Annie walks up to me. "So, we're going to London! Pretty cool, huh?"

"Oh, good. I knew you would make it," I say, glad for the distraction and also to know I'll have a friend on this journey with me. "That's *so* awesome. Who else is going?"

"Oh, it's the usuals and a few unusuals. We'll be quite a group. You'll see. First rehearsal is Monday after school. In fact, Mr. Collins said we're going to meet every other day after school until finals week."

"No shit, really?"

"Yes, really. This is going to be hardcore, Roman."

I peer at the list, now that only a few students are standing in front of it, and notice Max's name is not there.

Annie pulls over a short, round-faced, pretty African-American girl with a head full of tight braids. It's the girl I bumped into just earlier. "Hey, Jasmine, congrats. We're going to have a blast."

Jasmine smiles and nods at Annie. "I'm really excited!"

Annie points at me. "Do you know Roman? He's going, too."

"Yeah, I saw that," she says and turns away to talk to a group behind us.

"What's up with her?" I ask Annie.

"Oh, don't worry about it. She's got to warm up to you is all."

While I am not exactly worried about it, I do feel unsettled by the vibes Jasmine is throwing my way. I tell myself to shake it off as I head to my locker.

It's been a long month of having to be chauffeured everywhere because of my busted ankle. Now that I'm finally mended and the weather is actually decent, it's freeing not to have to text Mom or Grandma, "please pick me up," every time I need to get home from school.

I look forward to walking home in the sunshine as I sort out my thoughts about what comes next.

CHAPTER FORTY-SIX

"Mom, something big happened in school today," I say the second I walk in the door. She is sitting on the couch in the family room, reading a magazine.

"Okay, I think I know where this is going," she says slowly. "So, the poem? You won?"

"Yeah! I'm going to England. I guess my poem got a lot of points from the judges and maybe from the other kids, too. Annie's going, too. Claire's sister. And a bunch of kids I don't know. Plus Mr. Collins and one of the English teachers who grew up in London, Ms. Mann." The words come fast. I try to slow my thoughts down. There is so much I want to get out.

"Wow. Well, this is big news. I know you mentioned how everyone who's going needs to raise money for the trip. You'll have to figure that out. I think the neighbors could use some dog walking. We'll need to come up with some other ideas, too. There's a lot to do," Mom says, rambling on as she avoids the obvious.

"What about—"

"Yes, I know." She sticks her palm in front of my face to interrupt. "I'm already working on getting in touch with Marcel. He has a Facebook page. I will send him a message first thing tomorrow. Now that we know you are going to England, I think it may be less of a shock. Like why this is all happening now."

My heart is beating super-fast, and I sit down on the couch.

I need Mom to make this happen. I need to hear she is going to come through for me. That tomorrow she won't flake out on me.

"He looks good, Marcel. On Facebook, I mean," she says, and then she starts to babble as tears stream down her face. "It was really so intense, so incredible. I just sat with his Facebook page open and looked over and over again at the public posts and images. There aren't too many. And his page is all in French, which, you know, might as well be Greek—I don't know what it says. My parents have always believed I should tell him. But I just couldn't do it. I just was so scared, you know? I mean I love you so much, and then there's this guy I knew for a short time who's all the way in France. Geesh!"

It's weird that I'm half French, actually, and know nothing about France at all. Though I do like French fries and croissants.

Grandma walks into the room and sees Mom with her face all wet from crying. She turns into the kitchen and comes back holding a box of tissues, which she sets quietly on the side table. Mom grabs at the tissues and starts wiping her eyes and blowing her nose. Grandma sits down between the two of us.

"So?" Grandma says with warmth in her eyes, ready to either comfort or celebrate.

Before she can ask any more, I blurt out, "Good news, Grandma! I made it. I'm going to England. The judges really liked my poem."

"Of course they did, honey," she gushes, being all grandma-y. "Well, isn't this something?" She sets her left hand on mom's leg and then wraps her right arm around me. "I was wondering when this day would come."

CHAPTER FORTY-SEVEN

M onday after school, the eight of us meet in Mr. Collins's Spoken Word classroom. We sit in a circle of chairs and introduce ourselves.

Annie

Me

Jasmine

Desmond

Kamara

T.J.

Shivani

Emma

Kamara and I are the two freshmen in the group. Shivani and Jasmine are sophomores, and the rest of the group are juniors.

Mr. Collins tells us the first order of business for each of us is to secure passports, if we do not have them, which we must apply for in the next week to make sure they arrive in time. I'll need Mom to help me get this worked out pronto.

Then Mr. Collins talks money.

"I've done this before, raising funds for a trip like this. It's not as hard as you may think," he says. "We are working with a travel agency that books most of our school-led student groups. They'll get us a great deal on airfare and the hotel.

"The good news is I've already arranged for a generous grant from the Alumni Association that should cover about one-third of our expected costs. This week, I'll put that down as a deposit with the travel agency to go and book our flights. As I noted on the commitment sheet, each of you will need to contribute $400 to help offset the hotel room and excursions. If that's a hardship, talk to me privately, and we can work out a longer payment plan. As a group, we also need to raise $8,000. We reached that goal a few years ago, when we brought a group to Scotland, so I know we can do it again."

The next hour we sit and talk logistics: GoFundMe, car wash, bake sale. We throw out ideas like raffling off something cool or doing a Poetry on the Spot at the high school. Someone suggests we do it in Scoville Park, as well, and charge $5 for writing people their own personal poems. Kamara's grandma lives at a nursing home a block from the high school and says her mom told her maybe we could perform our poetry for the residents there to raise some money.

In short, we are going to be busy raising bucks.

I figure maybe I can send Kirk the GoFundMe link. We've been texting a few times a month, and Mom had me call him on his birthday, April 5. We talked for more than ten minutes about my life and his latest movie project he's about to film in Hawaii.

I told him how much I liked his newest movie, *Knight*, about the early days of Nike, which I saw one snowy Sunday afternoon with Grandpa and Mom. He filmed it partly in Canada, though the setting was Portland, Oregon. It came out to so-so reviews, and Mom said it did so-so in the theaters. I know he was disappointed. He was expecting big box office numbers, and I had heard him mention the words "Academy Award nomination" a few times.

That could still happen, but I know enough to keep those hopeful thoughts to myself unless something actually does pop up worth celebrating.

CHAPTER FORTY-EIGHT

The next day after school, I walk in the front door to see Grandma and Mom sitting on the family room sofa, talking intently. Mom turns to look at me. I do a double take. She looks really different. I swear she's morphing into a suburban mom. She has cut her hair so it hits above her shoulder and is wearing a long, black top over black and tan tie-dyed tights.

"Honey, what do you think?" she asks, shaking her head back and forth a few times so her hair whips around her neck "I went to my old hairdresser, Tommaso. I told him I wanted something different, and I that's what I got. He whacked off, like, six inches."

I shrug. "It's fine, Mom," I say. I think it makes her look older. Who knows, maybe that's what she's going for.

Grandma excuses herself from the sofa quietly and settles herself with a book in a chair nearby.

"Sit down, Roman," Mom says as she slides over on the sofa.

I drop my backpack on the carpet and plop down heavily next to her.

Mom spits out exactly what I was hoping she'd say. "Roman, I did it. I talked to Marcel. I told him about you. And I told him about the Spoken Word competition. We were on the phone for an hour, and I told him everything."

"Wow, Mom. This is huge!" I smile at her. She actually did it! I have so many questions swimming around in my head, I don't know where to begin. "What did he say?"

"Oh, honey. What *didn't* he say? I cried, he cried. He told me he had read about me and Joel. I guess it was in social media over there, so I couldn't escape that part even."

"Mom, he must have been so pissed when you told him about me."

"Yes. That's true. After I told him, there was stone-cold silence. I sat there on the phone while he didn't say a word. And then, boy, did I get an earful. Which I deserved. But he also acknowledged how young we were and that we've both grown up a lot since those days on the cruise ship."

"He wants me to mail him buckets of pictures. And he wants to come to London. For the competition. He wants to be there. He said he would fall apart if he didn't know that you'd be over there soon. The fact that you made this happen because you want to see him—it just made him less angry about the situation and more hopeful about how this will all unfold." She's all puffy around her eyes, although it's obvious she put makeup on to try and hide it. She really did cry big time.

"Yes, that's what I think, too, Mom. That's cool."

"He told me he has so much to think about, but first he wants to sit with all this news and write you a letter. He thinks that would be best—for you to read it and always have it. Then maybe figure out how this all works next."

"A letter?" It seems so old school. I remind myself that the generations before us did write letters. I hope he's not one of those Luddites or something. That was one of the words I learned from doing crossword puzzles with Grandpa. It means people who don't use technology. I hope he isn't one of those. But... he wants Mom to mail him pictures? He's writing a letter? My mind churns. Who is Marcel? What's his deal?

"Mom, is Marcel normal? Maybe he's a wacko?"

"Marcel is not a wacko, Roman," she snaps. "I know this situation is weird and unusual, but that doesn't mean he's those things."

"I am sure he is a perfectly wonderful man," Grandma interjects. She's been observing us closely, a closed hardcover book on her lap.

We both look at her and then at each other. Mom bites her bottom lip as we each stifle a laugh. Leave it to Grandma to break the tension. I start to climb down from my mountain of worry.

"Well, I'm going to see about dinner," she says, excusing herself.

"And I'm off to go lie down for a bit. I'm completely exhausted," Mom says as she stands up and then leans over and kisses me on the cheek. "This was the second time in a year I've been chewed out by a man."

"Mom, that is so fricking sad."

"Okay, I know. Give me some credit, Roman. I'm cleaning up my messes."

"Now you just have to stop making them," I say with conviction. "I can't take anymore."

"Trust me," she adds, "I can't, either."

I have so many questions I want answers to. Is he married? Does he have more kids? What's his job? Doe he still play saxophone? Has he ever been to Chicago? But I can see I won't get these answered today.

She walks away, leaving me alone on the sofa. I pull out my iPhone and scroll through my calendar to June 14.

Under Add Event, I type:

Meet My Dad.

CHAPTER FORTY-NINE

Saturday morning, I wake up at 10:30. The first thought that comes to mind is the same one I've had rolling around in my head for days. I have to—scratch that—I *want* to get Claire up to speed about what Grandpa called at the dinner table last night my "turning point" and "moment of truth."

Still lying on my stomach, I grab for my cell phone and roll over to text Claire I need to talk about some family stuff that's come up. She responds right away.

KK. Noon?

Scoville Park?

She texts back a smiley face, and soon we are sitting in the sunshine on the massive grass lawn in front of the library, her bike resting nearby. She starts to pull at the blades of grass and then looks over at me.

"What's up, Roman. Is everything okay with your mom?"

"Yes, that's all fine. It's just that something really, really big has happened."

"Oh my god. You're moving back to L.A. soon, aren't you?" She sounds serious with a bit of fear in her voice.

"Um, no. That's not it. It's something huger," I say. "It's about my father."

"Your father?" Then she sits quietly, watching me with her crystal-blue eyes.

I blurt it out. All of it. I throw down the whole insane story that is my life.

When I'm done, she looks at me, shell-shocked. "Wow." Then, a bit louder, she repeats, "Wow. How are you feeling about all this with Marcel?"

"Mostly I feel psyched about it. It's like, all of a sudden, what I've been thinking about my whole life is happening."

"I know. That's really, really cool. It's really exciting, Roman. You're not some boring American like the rest of us. You're international!" She laughs.

"That's true. It's funny because I signed up to take Spanish when I moved here. Living in L.A., that's the second language out there. Now I'm thinking I should switch to French next year, right?"

Claire leans back on her elbows in the grass and trains her eyes my way. "Um, duh. You have to do that. You could have some adorable French grandma who doesn't speak a word of English."

Now it's my turn to sit silently. All these years, I haven't thought past the idea that I have a father who lives in France. Leave it to Claire to further crack open my world.

I meet her gaze. *Man, I really like this girl!*

I lean down and kiss her. Our lips linger together. Hers are soft.

I flop back on my elbows alongside her, brushing her arm with mine.

"Who else knows about this?" she asks quietly.

"Nobody. I mean my family, of course. And Mr. Collins. My mom and I talked to him, to make sure he'd be on board, if I did get to London."

"Yeah, I bet he was awesome about everything," she says. "So, does Zuzu know?"

"Well, it was her idea in the first place," I answer honestly. "That's really why I decided to enter the competition."

Maybe I shouldn't have said that last part. Claire is always sensitive about anything to do with Zuzu. But it's the truth.

We sit quietly for a long while, our forearms touching and all but Velcroed together.

"I'm glad you told me about this," she finally says.

"Yeah," I say. "Me, too."

CHAPTER FIFTY

I walk home, trying to process the marching orders Mr. Collins threw out to the eight of us after school today. Getting ready for this competition is going to be a pain in the ass. On top off all the writing, rehearsing, raising money, and planning for London, school is crushing me with a bunch of end-of-the year crap piled on top of studying for finals. There's a lot of important homework being thrown my way, too, so I can't just pick what I want to get done. It's miserable. To survive, I have to do something I'm not too great at: be uber-organized.

Mr. Collins explained that, along with each of us reciting our solo piece alongside some of London's best teenage poets at the Friday night showcase, we are going to perform two group pieces in London to close out the Roundhouse Poetry Slam that Saturday. He wants us to team up in two groups of four and work together to come up with a performance full of movement and emotion.

"I would like to see one group piece have to do with summer and the other to be a take on winter," he said. "Please write a poem about both and bring them in on Monday. We'll start refining them by working together in the computer lab. Then, we will break off into two groups depending on how the poems work together."

I think about the first poem I wrote when Mr. Collins came into Mr. Katz's classroom, the one about me falling on my butt on black ice. I figure I can try to punch up that one for winter and then put all my time into writing something cool about summer, which is my favorite season anyway.

Seconds after I enter the kitchen door, Grandma walks in and asks, "How was school today?"

I drop my backpack on the floor next to the kitchen table. "Rough, Grandma. I have a bunch of Spoken Word stuff to do, and I was up until 1 a.m. writing a paper. I need sleep!"

"Roman, dear, I watch you very work hard. You have a full plate. But I also see you being very happy here. Am I right?"

"I *do* like it here." I try to cover my mouth to hide a yawn.

She smiles and reaches out for my hand, giving it a squeeze. "You've made wonderful friends and become so involved at the high school. It's a joy for your grandparents to see that."

I shrug. "I know Mom is set on L.A., so I guess I can deal with us going back next year."

"Is that what you really want, though? To go back?"

"I would stay in a second, instead of starting all over again. I love L.A., but this has been good, too, you know?" I am surprised at how quickly those words spill out.

I yawn big. Grandma takes the hint and walks toward the back door, mumbling something about grocery shopping. I slog upstairs and fall straight into my bed. I was already tired. Now, thanks to Grandma, my brain is fried from thinking too much.

CHAPTER FIFTY-ONE

After working together in the computer lab and reading aloud our newly minted poems, it turns out Jasmine, Desmond, Shivani, and I find a way to mash together our four poems about summer in a way that's entertaining and engaging.

Today, all of us are in our first full practice mode. The room swirls with the rhythms of eight voices, sounds of winter and summer clashing and careening over one another. The eight of us try to find our way through the tangle of meanings on display.

I love my poem on summer. I worked so hard on it that I gave up having a social life last weekend. Desmond's poem is the best of all of ours, but he keeps complaining about how dumb it sounds.

"I think it's a good poem," I say to him straight on. He shakes his head to cast off my approval.

All of a sudden, he says loudly to the whole group, "I think we should ditch the whole summer and winter theme. We should do something more intense. Like performing 'where I'm from' would be so much more interesting. Don't you think?" He looks around at our faces.

A handful of heads nod in tandem, like puppets. Now, no one wants to do the winter and summer poetry. I get that it wasn't one of Mr. Collins's best ideas.

"Let's try it," T.J. says.

"I agree," adds Annie.

I am outnumbered, so I sit silently. Clearly, everyone else in the group wants to switch directions.

Desmond walks across the hall to Mr. Collins's office, where he is working at his desk, and says loudly, "Mr. C, can we talk to you a minute?"

Mr. Collins steps away from his desk, oblivious to the mutiny going on across the hall, and asks from the door frame, "What's up?"

"Hey, Mr. Collins, how about we drop the summer-winter sh—" Desmond stops himself, cracking a smile. "Stuff. We want to do brand-new group pieces for the Roundhouse show."

Mr. Collins takes a few paces into the room and looks around at our expectant faces. "You're the ones who are going to get on stage," he says. "What do you propose doing?"

"Well, we really like this idea. We want people to know where we are from," Desmond explains.

"So, you want to start from scratch? Rewrite your poems?"

Seven heads nod affirmatively.

Personally, this is probably the last subject matter I would ever choose to write about, much less perform in front of Marcel.

I refuse to consider myself screwed. There's got to be a way to play this new theme so it's no big deal. I just have to figure out what that is.

"Okay then, get cracking," he says. "You have a lot of work to do, so get to it."

CHAPTER FIFTY-TWO

I'm hanging out in Nick's basement with Claire and a bunch of Nick's friends. She lives down the street from Nick, and they've been friends since kindergarten. *Everyone* likes going to his house, because he's got the coolest basement, with a 3D TV and a poker table. Also, ping-pong and pool tables, plus a whole kitchen setup including a freezer packed with pizzas and ice cream.

Claire and I root around and find a stash of Klondike bars. We sit on the sofa, eating them and trying to catch the drips before they fall onto the fake leather. She eats hers so slowly, it softens into a huge, melting blob, and she has to abandon it in the garbage and then unstick her hands in the sink.

Homes don't have basements in L.A., and there is something I am learning to love about hanging out with my friends underground. It's like we're in our own private cave, while the adults stay in their own space upstairs. We've entered the no-parent zone.

"How's rehearsals going for London?" Claire asks after we've played ping-pong and watched the end of *Finding Nemo* on TV, which is mind-blowing in 3D, by the way.

"I think okay. Though two of the kids are dissing everything I say about our group piece. They don't seem to like me much."

"Let me guess—Desmond and Jasmine? Did you know they are sister and brother, by the way?"

"Yes, I figured that part out." Then I sit up straight, wanting to hear more. "How'd you know they're the ones who don't like me?"

"Well, Annie told me they said some stuff. Don't be shocked. I mean look at it from their side. The rich kid from L.A. transfers into our school and crushes it right away with Spoken Word. They've been working at this for years, so they're thinking you're, well, privileged."

I'm pissed. "Well, first, you know I'm not rich, so that's stupid of people to say. And second, what, like I didn't earn it?"

"No, that's not it. Everyone thinks your poems are really good. You earned the spot for sure. Oh, I don't know, it's just that you made it seem too easy, like what was in the water out in L.A. or something? Most of us have to work a lot harder to write even halfway good poems."

"So, now I'm going to London with people who don't like me? That's shitty."

"Don't worry about it now. Just win them over with your Roman charm," Claire says.

"Or maybe I should invite them over to sit around and have Grandma's gluten-free, taste-free cookies and almond milk," I say, half-seriously. "Then they'd feel real sorry for me."

"You love to diss your grandma. But she's the best, and you know it."

"I know she is. But when I lived in L.A., there was this cook, Cora, and she would make me stuff like brownies with chocolate chips in them and all this great Mexican food covered in cheese. Now, I get oatmeal and wheat germ all the time. Did you know my grandma puts wheat germ in spaghetti sauce even?"

"Oh, that must taste awful."

"The awful part is that I didn't know it was in there until, like, last month. I caught her in the act one day, pouring it in, and now she's busted."

"Poor Roman," Claire teases.

"Yeah, I know. I have it rough."

She turns to Nick and Edward, who are chilling in front of some random show on Comedy Central, and challenges them to a ping-pong match.

"It's on," Nick says.

Claire and I pick up our paddles and stand next to each other. We warm up by hitting a bunch of good rallies that show we know our way around a ping-pong table and are pretty evenly matched.

We start slow but then pull out the stops and come back to win 17-21, 21-19, 21-18.

CHAPTER FIFTY-THREE

After two weeks, we enter the comfort zone. We've stuck with our two original groups, but we have a much better product to perform at Roundhouse. Desmond was right. I actually wrote a poem that, not to brag or anything, got snaps all around. Mr. Collins called it "mighty powerful."

All four of our poems kick ass now, but the choreography isn't working yet, at least not for me.

Jasmine nominated herself our choreographer, putting movement to our words, and she's been getting help from an alum named Chelsea, who pops into our practices from time to time.

They act like it's their way or the highway, but, still, I have my standards. I draw the line at some jazz-hands idea Chelsea dreams up. Luckily, Desmond backs me up on that one.

"So here," says Chelsea, "when you say 'I love reading, but pages I study for school are not worth the life of a tree,' I want you all to stick your hands up like a tree."

And from there it just all goes to hell. I feel like yelling at the top of my lungs during practice, "*Hello*! I'm a Spoken Word poet, not a dancer."

But I don't.

Instead, I do a stiff imitation of a tree and get properly yelled at by everyone in my group. Then we have more weird actions to memorize, prayer hands, and something called spin up and spin down… All done in unison.

"Try to be in sync, Roman," Jasmine says slowly and loudly in my direction, like she's talking to a child.

"Roman, you need to be fully enthused about these movements," Chelsea says.

"Just be smooth, man," says Desmond.

Even Shivani picks on me with some acid stares.

"Dancing's not in my DNA," I say, defending myself. "I can't help it."

"Just try harder, dude," Desmond replies.

So, I do. I don't like it. But I get a little less robotic at our next practice.

To let off steam, I complain to Zuzu, Claire, and even Annie.

"Why can't we just be low-key? Everything is so over the top," I grumble. "A powerful line needs focus, not…" I demonstrate an example of what I just don't like—the tree branch move, for starters. "I've done group pieces before. But this is just insanely frickin' girly."

Zuzu says, "Suck it up. The stupid moves won't kill you."

Claire's advice? Try to "go with the flow."

Annie tells me I have to "live in the moment and not worry so much."

I'm tempted to bring my issues to Mr. Collins, but I don't expect him to care, either.

What are my options?

I swallow my pride. It's a small price to pay for this whole London experience.

By the last rehearsal, I'm almost passable. At least Shivani, Desmond, and Jasmine stop complaining and giving me dirty looks.

After spending countless hours together, it was inevitable.

We're all growing on one another.

CHAPTER FIFTY-FOUR

I walk in the back door after a grueling Spoken Word practice to a quiet house. I grab a bag of Sun Chips from the pantry, pour some lemonade from the fridge, and sit down at the kitchen table. It's one of the house rules that's been hardest to stick to: no eating in front of the television. And no eating in my room.

I notice a letter smack in the center of the table with a bunch of stamps on it and a square, blue sticker that reads *PAR AVION*. I abandon my snack when I see the envelope is addressed to me. In the left corner it says in black script "M. Bucher" and a return address from Arles.

My letter. From Marcel. My heart races as I turn it over and slide my finger under the fold to force it open.

Inside is a white notecard with black handwriting that fills the rectangular page and three color photos. I stare at the first photo, which is of an elderly couple dressed formally; he wears a dark suit and she is in a bright-green dress; they both sit facing the camera with wine glasses between them on the table and stare out with half-smiles. I flip the photo over. In blue script, it reads, *My parents, Sophia and Bernard Bucher.*

The second photo, I know instantly, is a picture of him. He's posed in front of clear blue waters that stretch out behind him on what I realize is a cruise ship, and he's smiling into the camera, his right hand resting on the railing behind. He wears a black, long-sleeve, button-down shirt belted into tan pants. I wonder if that's what he wore when he performed on the ship.

I look closely at the photo. He's skinny and tan, and his long brown hair is messy and windblown. I hold the picture tighter, searching for clues in his face, his stance. Maybe that's my chin, too? My nose? On the back, *1998* is written in the same blue ink. The year I was born.

The third photo is him in what looks like present time, standing outside a stone building with bright-blue shutters. His head is almost swallowed up by a huge bush behind him with blue flowers. It winds up from the ground and explodes in every direction. Here, he's just as skinny as in the earlier photo, but his hair looks shorter, though still longish. On the back, he has written *Arles*.

I study the photos for a long time and then stick them carefully inside my gray notebook. Then I turn my attention to the note, which has been written in careful, black, block letters.

Roman,

I am blessed to have been your father since the minute you were born. I wish I could have been there to guide you. I wish I could have been able to share in your joys, to help you through your sorrows, and to show you all that fathers teach their young sons. That was not to be. Now we have the chance to make our own memories. Mon fils, you are so very present in my heart and in my mind. Forever you will be in my thoughts and prayers.

À bientôt.

Chaleureusement,

Marcel

P.S. Reach out when you feel ready. My cell is #33 4 90 49 55 5. Call, Skype, or text anytime. I use WhatsApp to text international. It's free.

If, one day, my house is on fire or there is a hurricane barreling my way, if I ever have to leave in a panic and can only grab frantically for one thing, I know what it would be. If you'd asked me ten minutes ago, I would have probably said my computer. I would want to take my laptop. I wouldn't have known or cared about any of my stuff.

Now, I do.

I place Marcel's note underneath the photos and close my notebook then take it with me upstairs and put it on the nightstand, next to my bed. I wish I could keep this letter and these photos just for myself. But I know Mom will want to see them.

I'll show them to her when she asks, but not because I want to share them. I'll show her because the more she learns about Marcel and his life, the more she will understand me.

CHAPTER FIFTY-FIVE

It takes me a few days to get my nerve up. But then I just do it. Mom asked me, after reading Marcel's letter and seeing the photos, what I was going to do, and I told her I'd figure it out. Which I have.

I open up the WhatsApp app on my iPhone—I set it up the same night I got Marcel's note.

I send the message.

> *I got your letter and photos. Thanks.*

I practically glue my eyes to the screen, waiting for his reply. Hours go by and I don't get anything back. I check the world clock and realize it is 3 a.m. in France. I give up my vigil and hit the sheets.

When I wake up, I see he messaged me back in the middle of the night, which, in France, is the morning. It's all a bit fuzzy.

> *Hi, Roman. I am so glad to hear from you. How is your practice proceeding?*

Funny text, right? So, from there, we begin messaging every day.

I think we both want the same thing. Not jumping onto Skype or FaceTime. It's doesn't feel right. What does feel right is writing on our own private platform about small, safe topics.

At least until we can be together in the same room. That's when it'll get real.

CHAPTER FIFTY-SIX

The eight of us are packed into the Spoken Word office with Mr. Collins. Since there aren't enough chairs, Jasmine leans against Mr. Collins's large, pockmarked wood desk that is piled with papers and books. I'm propped against the wall as Mr. Collins walks in holding a green folder.

"Great job, crew, on the fundraising," he announces, plucking a piece of paper from the folder and rattles off the numbers:

"$5,345—GoFundMe. Awesome! $460—carwash. Well done. $210—Poetry on the Spot. Other donations—$325. So, we're at $6,340.

"We've still got two weeks to meet our goal," he adds. "We can be okay with where we're at. We'd maybe have to cut out some of the tourist sites and skip seeing a play in London. But we'll have more practice time and free time to explore, which is great, too." He looks around at us. "Thoughts?"

Selling candy is something he nixes; he says other groups in our school do that. We decide to double down on our GoFundMe. I've been waffling about sending the link to Kirk. I was all set to do it, but since some kids have this image of me as the spoiled L.A. kid, getting a donation from Kirk would only fuel that. And then there's the whole dad deal. I realize I need to step up and tell Kirk about Marcel and London.

That night, I spend thirty minutes writing and rewriting a text to Kirk about Marcel, London, and the GoFundMe site. But there is just too much backstory now. I've kept Kirk in the dark too long. I realize it isn't fair to try to explain in a text everything that's happened in my life.

Closing my door, I sit heavily on my bed and lean into my phone to text Kirk.

Hi. Are you free to talk?

He texts back quickly:

Sure. Call me in ten.

I watch the minutes on my phone tick by. Should I rehearse what I want to say? Or wing it? I go for the second one.

My heart jumps when the ten minutes is up. It beats quickly as I navigate to my Favorites bar and hit Kirk's name.

"Hey, Champ," he says, answering on the first ring. "What's the latest?"

Well, he asked. So, I take a deep breath and then fill him in, starting at the beginning with Mr. Collins and Spoken Word. I tell Kirk about Marcel, about the competition, about London, about the fundraising. Then I shut up to wait for his response.

He doesn't hesitate. He tells me he's happy I've connected with Marcel. He's excited I've discovered writing, saying obviously I have a gift for it.

Then he asks, "So, what is this Spoken Word?"

I start to ramble, giving a long-winded answer from the top of my head. I want Kirk to really *get* what it is and how it connects to his world.

"It's poetry, but you don't read it. You perform it," I say. "We tell our stories. First, we memorize them, and then we stand up on stage by ourselves or, sometimes, in a group, and we have to project our voices and all that acting stuff you taught me."

"Sounds like you found your own version of Hollywood in Chicago," he says. "I'm impressed."

He tells me he's thrilled I have this opportunity to do my poetry *and* meet Marcel in London. And then he asks me to text him the GoFundMe link.

Man, it's hard work being me, I think as I hang up the phone and text him the link with a few emojis added on to say thanks. I'm happy I did the right thing and Kirk responded like I had hoped he would.

Or maybe not.

Two days later and the GoFundMe total hasn't budged more than $60.

Maybe I went too far?

Three days out, same thing.

Maybe Kirk is really pissed as hell that I asked him for the money. Did I blow it with him because of Marcel? Did I ask too much?

I tell myself not to worry. Still, in the back of my head, worry lurks. I can't shake it.

As I am walking to school the following morning, my phone buzzes. It's from Kirk.

I realize it's, like, 6 a.m. out in L.A., which is when Kirk usually begins his day. I picture him sitting at the kitchen table with his coffee and the *New York Times*. He doesn't read the *Los Angeles Times*. He says it has too much fluff.

Nervous, I open up his text.

All done. Sorry for the delay. Cora wanted to help out, too.

I fire up the GoFundMe app on my phone and see right away a new anonymous donation for $1,500. Cora's $25 is listed underneath.

I quickly lean into my T-shirt sleeve to wipe away a tear that slips down my cheek without permission. I'm half a block away from school, so I pull myself together and stick my phone back in my pocket.

CHAPTER FIFTY-SEVEN

It rains most of the afternoon, leaving a damp mist in the air. Water drips down from the trees, and puddles dot the sidewalk as Zuzu and I walk toward my house after school. I fill her in about all that's going on with Marcel and Kirk and the London group. There's a lot to tell.

"And you're welcome," she says after I finish my long-ass story.

"Yeah, whatever," I grumble. "Or maybe this is all your fault."

"Your life was a soap opera before you came here, so don't put that on me." Zuzu jumps over a puddle I step quickly around. "How's it going with Marcel? So, you're texting?"

"Yeah. It's awkward. He texts me every day, asking about my poetry and how I'm doing. I'm always checking my phone now. I feel stupid when there's no text and then nervous when there is," I admit. Zuzu is the best therapist no money can buy.

"Then maybe don't text anymore. Just wait until you meet him. That's what counts anyway."

"I can't just stop answering his texts. I get that he wants to make up for lost time and all." This back and forth with Marcel has my stomach pretty much tied into knots. It takes me off my game and puts my head in this strange place where I can't stop thinking about what I've done and what comes next.

"He wants what's best for you, too, right?"

"How do I tell Marcel his texts stress me out, though?" That's something I've been wondering about lately.

"Contrary to popular belief, I don't know everything." She shrugs. "Why don't you ask your mom? She got you into this whole thing."

"No, not really. You did, remember? You already took credit for this whole thing."

"Okay. True. But what I'm saying is have your mom tell him how hard this is."

Zuzu's phone buzzes and she pulls it from her pocket to check her latest message.

As we continue walking, she types an answer quickly, using both thumbs. She's a master texter. For a few minutes, I walk beside her silently as she texts back and forth with, I assume, Jackson.

I see a big puddle ahead but don't warn her. As we both wade into it, her white tennis shoes get completely drowned. I slosh through the shallow edge.

"Shit, Roman," she says, looking down at her soaked feet and sliding her phone back in her jeans pocket. "You suck!"

I laugh.

"Good thing we're almost at your house. I need to borrow some socks."

That night, I actually take Zuzu's advice and ask Mom to tell Marcel I'm really busy with the Spoken Word rehearsals and getting ready for my trip. That I'm super, super-excited to finally meet him but also feeling weirded out about the whole thing. The daily texts are both awesome and stressing me out at the same time. She gets it right away.

"Yes, of course, sweetheart," she says brightly, seeming so happy to help lighten my load. "Let me explain to him how overwhelmed you are now. I'll give him all the details about the Roundhouse Poetry Slam."

When I wake up the next day, Marcel has sent me a text:

Roman, your mom filled me in on your travels and the poetry slam on Saturday. I am planning for our dinner. I am over the moon with happiness to see you. Have a safe trip.

I feel my stomach do a flip as I read it. I want this to work more than I've wanted anything in my whole life.

I text back simply,

Me, too. Thanks.

CHAPTER FIFTY-EIGHT

Mom has been on my case for the past two days to pack. Mr. Collins told us each to bring two Spoken Word performance outfits and an umbrella, "just in case." Other than that, it's summer, so figuring out what I need is not going to be rocket science.

"Mom, chill. I can throw my stuff together in five minutes," I tell her, not once or even twice but three times.

The day before our trip, she comes close to having a heart attack over what she says is my "failure to organize." So, it's not a huge surprise when she walks in and sits on my bed the minute I open my bedroom door at 11:00 the next morning. It's still six hours before we have to meet at the high school and take the school van to O'Hare Airport for our 8:30 evening flight to London's Heathrow Airport.

"Mom, what's up?" I ask her, playing along.

"Roman," she says, her voice tight like she's at the end of her last nerve. "Let's get you packed."

"Fine!" I'm as ready to get this over with as she is. Mom watches me start to jam the clothes I need into a square, black suitcase she stuck in the corner of my room days ago.

She walks out and returns seconds later carrying a blue shopping bag with the word Nordstrom printed on the side. Setting it down on my bed, she pulls out a pair of khaki pants, a dark-brown leather belt, and a white, button-down shirt with dark-blue stripes.

"I thought you could wear this when you perform. When you meet Marcel," she says quietly. I check the sizes and see she's got them right.

"These are great, Mom. Thanks," I say. And they actually are.

"I want to iron the shirt and pants before you pack them up, so I'll do that this morning."

We double-check I have my passport, phone charger adapter, and spending money — three twenty-dollar bills Grandma slipped my way and a handful of colorful twenty-pound notes we got at the bank.

"Well, I think you're in good shape for London," Mom announces, finally satisfied enough to go find the iron.

Okay, packing took twenty minutes, not five, but still. Parents can be so weird.

CHAPTER FIFTY-NINE

At the airport, after clearing security in Chicago, the eight of us sit in a circle on the blue carpet near our gate and share travel stories. Not even one of us has ever been on such a long flight.

"This is my first flight ever," says Kamara quietly. She walks over to the large glass window and stares out at the humongous plane. Turning back to us, she adds forcefully, "I don't feel too good. I hope I don't throw up."

"Well, don't sit next to me," says Shivani. She means it, too. You can tell.

"Hey, Kamara, don't worry. You've got this," Annie says, walking over and putting her arm around Kamara's shoulder. Together, they turn away from the plane and rejoin our circle on the floor. We still have an hour before boarding. T.J. takes out a deck of cards, and he, Desmond, Jasmine, and I play some low-key blackjack to pass the time.

Kamara ends up sitting on the aisle, next to my middle seat, on the flight.

"Here's your barf bag," I half-joke as I pull it out from the seat pocket and fling it on her lap.

"Oh, they have these? Then a lot of people must get sick!" She looks down nervously at the white bag.

"No, they don't," I say as a warning. "It's just in case." Now I'm worried.

She grips the arm rests and shuts her eyes during takeoff. Luckily for us both, she doesn't need to open the bag.

Minutes after the flight attendants clear our dinner trays, my classmates are fast asleep all around me. Between staying alert to the possibility of projectile vomit heading my way and the anticipation of all that lies ahead, I'm the last one awake. About halfway into the nine-hour flight, 4,000 miles from one continent to another (I Googled that waiting around at the airport), I finally nod off in my seat.

Our plane lands at Heathrow at 11:00 a.m. London time, which we quickly discover is only 5 a.m. in Chicago. That's our first reality check. Trailing our luggage behind us, we hike over to the Underground, a.k.a. the Tube, which is London's version of the subway. As we walk up the subway stairs into Piccadilly Circus, we get our second reality check: rain. While all of us have taken Mr. Collins's advice and packed umbrellas, none of us wants to spend our first moments in London peering out from beneath a thick, fabric dome.

We all stop at the busy street corner to stare at strange vehicles driving the wrong way down the wide streets.

"The black cars you see are the official London taxis," explains Ms. Mann, adding, "And, as you can see, not only do vehicles drive on the left, but the driver's seat is on the right. So, pay attention please, students." She quickly has to pull Kamara back from the curb before she nearly gets flattened by a red double-decker bus.

CHAPTER SIXTY

After dropping all our suitcases with the front desk clerk at our hotel, since it's too early for us to check in, Ms. Mann leads us into Covent Garden, which is *not* a garden, but *is* a market. We follow her downstairs to her favorite crêpe place.

Afterward, we wander over to the South Bank, where we stop to stare out at the River Thames. We've left the umbrellas back at the hotel and are all wettish from the misty rain, but we're *in London,* so nobody's complaining.

Annie stands next to me and grabs hold of the metal banister. We stare out at the handful of boats on the water and a massive Ferris wheel, the London Eye, visible in the distance. "Isn't this amazing?" she says. "Claire is so jealous!"

"I know. I try not to rub it in and send her too many pictures." Our whole group just took a bunch of selfies in front of something called Cleopatra's Needle.

"Hey, can I ask you a question?" Annie looks serious.

"Yeah. What's up?" I'm not sure where this is going.

"Your poem. It's really good, but it's so personal. Like, what did your mom say about it?"

Aha! Here is Annie telling me she understands what this trip means to me. I kinda figured Claire told her about my dad—there's no way that secret stayed between us. Even I get it's too huge. But I hope, I think, it's gone no further.

"I never showed it to my mom or my grandparents. I told them I wanted Spoken Word to be my thing. I haven't read them my poems or invited them to the showcases," I explain. "They've asked. It's just that the only way I can be real about what I write is if I know I won't have to explain myself to them."

"Yeah, I get it. I feel like asking my parents to back off sometimes, too. You know my poem about my dad and me walking the dog together? It's so embarrassing because my mom framed it and put it on a shelf in the family room."

"No way! That's what I mean. Parents can be insane." We both laugh.

I'm okay with Annie and, of course, Mr. Collins and Ms. Mann knowing about the weight I carry around London. Everyone else in our group thankfully seems to be clueless about what I don't want them to be clued in to.

Mr. Collins warned us we'd be tired this first day in London, but damn! We're all zombies by 5:30 and ready for bed. But the trick, we are told, is to stay up 'til we can crash at a "normal" bedtime, so we can wake up tomorrow ready to roll.

Finally, at 9:30, we're allowed to do just that, and after I throw on a clean T-shirt and boxer shorts, I burrow under the covers of my hotel room bed and fall asleep in two seconds. On the night table between my bed and T.J.'s, I set my iPhone alarm for a 7:30 a.m. wakeup call. We have to get our day started early, since it's jam packed.

CHAPTER SIXTY-ONE

After the eight of us manage to straggle down to the hotel lobby a little after 8:00 a.m., Ms. Mann asks, "Has anyone had an English breakfast? It really is the best way to get oneself over jet lag!"

"Is it vegetarian, Ms. Mann?" asks Shivani.

Ms. Mann laughs. "Well, part of it is. You'll want to stay away from the black pudding."

We sit around two pushed-together tables at a pub-like restaurant down the street from our hotel and order nine English Breakfasts and one eggs and hash browns for Shivani.

"You cannot eat that black pudding. So gross," Shivani says, scrunching up her face as she eyes her phone.

She passes the phone to Emma, who peers down and reads out loud, "Black pudding is a blend of onions, pork fat, oatmeal, flavorings, and blood (usually from a pig)."

The talk around the table shifts to who will even try it.

"It's really not bad," Ms. Mann says, coming to the defense of her country.

"When in Rome! You know," adds Mr. Collins. Then he flashes a grin my way.

"Oh, so now I have to try it?" I ask.

Our breakfasts arrive, and we poke around at the mushrooms, tomatoes, and beans then head straight for the more familiar eggs, toast, and hash browns. The black pudding isn't pudding at all. It looks like burned sausage patties.

Ms. Mann makes a point to eat her black pudding right away.

I cut into it and place a small piece on my tongue, chewing slowly. "It tastes like salty beef jerky," I say, unimpressed.

At the end of the meal, most of us have left the black pudding untouched on our plates.

"I know the point of being here is trying new things," says Kamara as we leave the restaurant. "But I just couldn't do it!" A few heads nod in agreement.

"I liked it," says T.J.

"You would," teases Emma, swatting his arm playfully. She has been flirting with him since our group became, well, a group.

After visiting the Palace of Westminster and then watching the very cool Changing of the Guards at Buckingham Palace, we are set loose in Trafalgar Square for lunch and shopping. The girls take off on their own mission to check out the street vendors, while T.J., Desmond, and I wander the narrow streets, looking at all the touristy crap for sale.

Later that afternoon, we meet a group of ten British high school students from Barbican Young Poets at a café on Brick Lane. We sit awkwardly with the ten of them on one side of the room and us on the other until Mr. Collins breaks the tension with food. It's Shivani's sixteenth birthday in a few days, and the barista steps into our posse and sets a cake lit with candles down on the table. We all sing "Happy Birthday" then eat the sugary sponge cake, which provides our group the jolt we need. Sorry, Ms. Mann, but the English Breakfast did *not* cure our jet lag.

It turns out the London students are super-friendly and soon we exchange a bunch of WhatsApp contacts with our new friends. We are going to be workshopping with them tomorrow morning.

Our group all downloaded WhatsApp to our phones during our last meeting in Mr. Collins's office, when we went over the trip itinerary. It was Ms. Mann's idea. I knew all about it already, though, since it's what I've been using to text with Marcel for weeks.

Two blonde British girls walk over and introduce themselves to me, Shivani, and T.J. The kind of short one puts out her hand and introduces herself as Lydia, and the slightly shorter one tells me her name is Rose.

Rose eyeballs me for an awkward few seconds and then turns and says not quietly to Lydia, "Doesn't he kinda look like Harry Styles?"

The next thing I know, T.J.'s elbow is jabbing me kinda hard in the side while Lydia and Shivani laugh.

So embarrassing.

I realize Claire can easily hear about everything that happens here in London. I don't need Annie to send her a text that I'm flirting with these London girls, which I am so *not*, and mess up what we have. I make my escape to a door that has the letters WC written on it, which I've learned is British-speak for Water Closet. At this point, I'm past caring that my quick exit is to a bathroom.

"Harry, you're so dreamy," Shivani says, putting her hands under her chin to bug me as we walk out the door onto the gray cobblestone street.

"*Ha.* So funny, Shivani," I reply.

T.J. comes to my defense. "Man, those girls think you're hot, but I get that you're not into them."

"No! I'm not." I start to pout.

To be honest, I've been told that same thing Rose blurted out a bunch of times. It never bothered me before. I mean why would it? But in front of this group, the stakes are higher. There's Claire, of course. Also, Harry's not a nickname I want to encourage.

Ms. Mann leads us enthusiastically along narrow, winding lanes. We have to rush to keep up with her. We climb onto a bus headed to Shakespeare's Globe Theatre to catch a performance of *Antony and Cleopatra*. After we've squeezed ourselves into the first few rows of seats, Ms. Mann tells us proudly we are about to experience one of Shakespeare's classic tragedies.

The eight of us stay poker-faced. My mind flashes to an image of actors in velvet costumes reciting dusty Old English. I believe I can safely speak on behalf of my classmates when I say that tragedy is the perfect word to describe the evening ahead of us.

CHAPTER SIXTY-TWO

The next morning, we arrive at Soho Theatre to spend two hours before our showcase workshopping with the Barbican Young Poets.

Later that evening, we'll be standing on stage in one of the Soho Theatre's performance spaces. We're each going to recite our individual poems, the ones we performed to get us here in the first place.

"Welcome to our Chicago friends!" their teacher, Mr. Taylor, begins. He sweeps his arm around the dingy rehearsal room. It's ringed with two rows of colorfully painted, beat-up metal chairs. "I want to start with a group exercise, so we can get to know one another better and to get our creative juices flowing." He then motions with his other arm to Mr. Collins, who has taken a seat next to Ms. Mann in the outer circle. "So, Patrick, what does Spoken Word mean to you?"

"Oh, I see I'm the guinea pig here. Okay," Mr. Collins says as he stands. "I can do that." He looks over to the ten British students seated across the room. "Spoken Word is poetry with attitude." His words burst with intensity. "It's a way for me to look at the world so I'm inspired by what I see. And what I see I want to share with you all in a way that you can understand it, too." He turns to Mr. Taylor. "Now, Bill, it's your turn."

"Not bad, Pat. Well, I was thinking it's *their* turn. I'll save mine for later. Now, I want to hear from you what Spoken Word means. But I want to hear it in a Spoken Word poem, of course. Let's work for twenty minutes and then do some sharing."

The room is mostly quiet, other than some whispering and cell phone dings. A clock on the wall ticks so loudly, I can't get my brain to focus on putting words to paper. I write some fluff about how reciting Spoken Word poetry is one of my superpowers. How it transforms boring words into action. Clichés—which I know Mr. Collins hates. In my defense, I have a lot on my mind.

Tomorrow is our big event at the Roundhouse, where we will perform our two group pieces in front of an audience that will really and actually include my real, actual dad.

Don't think this fact hasn't been there, in the back of my head, every second of this trip. It has sloshed around, fighting for space with the jet lag and all the mind-boggling experiences I'm having.

After I scribble some words and doodle some pathetic-looking stick figures on the page for what seems like a long time, Mr. Taylor asks us to share what we've written. One of his students, Isaiah, a big muscular guy with a huge, round face atop a thick neck, volunteers to go first. He stands in front of his chair and faces the twenty of us, reading with a commanding voice.

> *Spoken word taught me*
> *nouns are bones*
> *adjectives are fat*
> *and verbs are muscles*
> *meanings, I bend sheets of paper like yoga mats*
> *when I stretched syllables*
> *flip clichés till they are "other side of the pillow" cool.*
> *I keep my word count to a minimum like dietitians do*
> *calories.*
> *Like dialect on diets*
> *brevity only breaks a sweat for wit.*

The second hand on the wall clock loudly clicks over and over in its perpetual circle as the room is spellbound in silence. I'm in disbelief that this big, beefy guy has written something so frickin' clever.

I look over at T.J. and Desmond. One by one, I lock eyes with each of my team members. Are they thinking what I'm thinking? I'm hoping these London kids are not all poetry gods like Isaiah here. If they are, we're in trouble.

"Well done, Isaiah," Mr. Taylor says. "Okay, who's next? Why don't we hear from one of our American friends?"

Nobody is next. We all cast our eyes downward, so as not to attract Mr. Taylor's attention, not one of us wanting to follow that moment of excellence.

"I don't know how we top that, Mr. Taylor," says Ms. Mann, walking into the middle of our circle and coming to our rescue. "How about if we do some introductions and talk about our inspirations for the individual pieces we are going to perform later today?"

Sighs of relief fill the room. We move on to a boring go-around of whose poems mean what that devolves into talk about what sightseeing spots are next on our agenda. There is complete disbelief among the London students that our trip to their city doesn't include a Harry Potter Studio Tour.

"Yeah, Mr. Collins. What's up with that?" Jasmine asks, looking over at him and then Ms. Mann, who are back to observing from seats behind ours. Shivani and I follow her lead and playfully gang up on our two chaperones. Within a few minutes, we give up. Their harsh glares tell us it's time to move on from this topic.

During the last hour of our workshop, we chat excitedly with our English friends about all the cool things we've done and how gross that black pudding stuff is.

"How do you guys eat that?" asks Kamara.

"Oh, you mean blood pudding?" asks a student named Abeerah, who wears a hijab. "Muslims don't go near it."

"I'm Jewish, and we don't, either," says Emma. As the girls look at each other, I realize this could go badly. But then Abeerah nods in agreement, and Emma smiles brightly in her direction.

"Well, before we all leave, I want to tell you what Spoken Word means to me," Mr. Taylor says after watching Abeerah and Emma connect over their shared avoidance of anything pork. He stands in front of his seat near the door. "Spoken Word can take a room full of strangers, people who have the courage to stand up and share their stories, and turn it into one big, happy family. We look forward to hosting our American family later tonight and hearing those stories."

As we swarm out of the room, Shivani and Jasmine walk beside Mr. Collins and continue to try to convince him we should cancel our scheduled morning visit to the British Museum and instead head to the Warner Bros. Studio Tour for the Making of Harry Potter attraction.

Let's just say Mr. Collins is not pleased that we would want to throw aside a chance to experience what he calls "real history." Our Harry Potter campaign doesn't end well.

CHAPTER SIXTY-THREE

Later that night, we follow Mr. Collins and Ms. Mann into the ninety-seat performance space at Soho Theatre, where each Barbican Young Poet and Spoken Word team member will stand and recite an individual poem. A handful of what I assume are family members and friends are seated throughout the room. The first three rows are filled with high school students who talk loudly across one another. Their British accents make everything they say sound high class.

Mr. Collins ushers us up the wood stairs, where two rows of chairs face a single microphone at center stage. "You've worked really hard, and tonight is for you to have fun," he says as the eight of us take our seats alongside the ten London club members. I'm not so sure "fun" is the word I would choose to describe each of us reciting an intense poem while hearing more of the same.

It turns out he is right.

I have a great time. Most of all, I'm relieved. The Barbican Young Poets are pretty good, but they are not all poetry gods. I think we Americans make a pretty impressive showing. We followed Mr. Collins's Golden Rule and are one-hundred-percent invested in our delivery. Nobody screws up their poems even a little—though I'm not surprised, since we've practiced them a few dozen times.

As soon as the final British student, Rose, recites her last line, someone blasts music, and the British kids all jump from their seats and start dancing around. Emma grabs T.J. and joins in. Soon we're all letting out the nervous energy and emotions that sat heavily on stage. A bunch of students from the first rows run up the steps to join their classmates, sliding back the chairs.

Quickly, the stage is filled with bodies laughing and moving as the music fills the room. Lydia starts to dance with me, and I act kinda mean and turn away from her. But what can I do? Annie's right there, and these next twenty-four hours are the most important of my life. I don't need any more drama, thank you very much.

After a twenty-minute dance fest that Kamara and I mostly sit out, we head into the warm night to walk the four blocks to our hotel.

"Some of that wasn't English, Ms. Mann," Desmond tells her as we walk down Shaftesbury Street. "I had no idea what they were talking about half the time."

"It was the accents that got me," says Emma. "I mean, I liked a lot of their poetry when I understood it."

"Do you think they're saying the same things about us?" I ask, truly curious.

"I think you all did a wonderful job speaking clearly and slowly," says Ms. Mann. "If there were some British words you didn't know or dialects that were strong, let's use that as preparation for what to expect during the main event tomorrow night."

"Yeah, like Lydia used this word 'knackered'—what's that?" Annie asks Ms. Mann.

"Oh, that's how I think we all feel right now," she says. "Really, really tired."

"Amen to that," says Jasmine. "I'm totally knackered."

CHAPTER SIXTY-FOUR

We walk over to the Charing Cross Underground Station to catch a train to the Roundhouse Theatre for our grand finale. It's our last night in London. My "mates" are acting animated and relaxed, mingling comfortably with the energy of the people on the street as they breathe in the warm night air.

And then there's me. Mr. Quiet and Jumpy. Annie walks in my shadow, quietly channeling her moral support my way, as we head into the noisy auditorium. It teems with teenagers and families. The seats up front have been reserved for student performers, so the ten of us take over the second row.

Mr. Collins glances at the program booklet we were each handed when we walked in. He leans over to show us our names listed as featured guests, with the final two performances of the evening.

"That's huge!" Jasmine says, squirming in her seat with anticipation.

"There will be a lot of solo performances before you go on, so really soak in the stories you hear," he advises.

I turn around in my seat, knowing Marcel is out there among this sea of at least three hundred faces. I scan the room hopelessly and then, *bam*! I feel an electric charge as he stands up to wave quietly in my direction from eight rows away. He gives me a thumbs up.

I smile as my heart feels like it's going to explode through the roof. I send a quick wave back his way and sit down to calm my nerves. I tell myself, "I've got this." I try to cool my anticipation about being in the room with Marcel by running through all my poetry, although I know it like the back of my hand.

But the words are not there. Where have they gone? *This could be bad*, I think. Will they come back when I need them? Which is fucking soon!

Two hours of student performances fly by, but I don't know what anyone says or does. I stare at the movements on stage while my head races with expectations and hopes and fears that jump quickly in and out of my head. I look at the exits and consider an escape, even though I know there is no place to go.

But up. Because now it's our turn. Desmond is sitting next to me and he nudges my arm. I stand to follow Shivani on stage. I feel sick. Trapped. I'm going to bomb. My brain can't focus, I can't do it. I can't I can't I can't.

I must. I know I must. What's my choice? *Shit*! This is so much harder than I thought it would be.

Mr. Collins walks up to me and touches my shoulder. "Roman, you okay?" We walk up the stairs to the stage side by side.

"No, not really," I answer glumly.

"You don't have to go up there," he whispers.

I grab onto his words and start to nod and turn around. But a voice in my head fights back. I came all the way to London to do *this* and do it in front of Marcel. *This is my moment,* the voice says.

"I can do it," I answer crisply with a tight grin, trying to reassure him. He pats me on the arm and turns away. I stick close to my group, saying, "It's just three minutes." No biggie.

I stand between Shivani and Jasmine and look out at the lights and the rows and rows of people who have trained their eyes on us. One of them is Marcel.

My mind is a blur. I hear Shivani start her poem. I follow her movements, the bending right, the stupid spinning thing I vowed twenty times not to do. And I know I am up next.

I wait for my cue. Shivani steps away from the mic and then stands still. She looks expectantly at me, and I slide over to the spot in the center of the stage. I open my mouth before I realize I have nothing to say. There are no words in my brain, no sounds on my tongue. There is a heavy, awkward silence around me.

After a few missed beats that seem like eternity, Jasmine moves closer and belts out my first line. *"Now you see me..."*

Oh, duh! I think, as my mind kicks into gear. Suddenly, everything is familiar.

I jump in. I've got my groove. I am back. From deep down in my gut, the words jump up to my brain like old friends. I'm standing tall, and my voice bellows out toward the audience…

> *…or you don't.*
> *Chicago born*
> *a toothless wonder*
> *I cut my teeth in L.A.*
> *sun surf sand.*
> *Then SLAM!*
> *Sharpened them up in Chicago*
> *snow ice sometimes sun*
> *all the time*
> *keeping my monster hook shot*
> *in my back pocket*
> *but slipping into the part of*
> *beat poet*
> *for good measure.*
> *And on the wings of*
> *Words Spoken*
> *London, here I stand*
> *teeth bared,*
> *awestruck*
> *at the part I play.*

Jasmine picks up now with her smooth, silky words. As a group, we huddle, we snap our fingers, and we turn around in a slick, singular spin. We own it as Desmond adds his golden touch to finish our act with sentences that splash down heavy and deep.

Walking down the steps from the stage back to our seats, Jasmine gives me a look. "What happened to you?" she whispers.

"Yeah, sorry. I blanked. Thanks for saving me. I fucked up."

"Oh, it wasn't that bad. I thought you were having a stroke though." She smiles.

CHAPTER SIXTY-FIVE

After the final performance, where the other team crushes it on stage with their totally mushy group piece that makes your teeth hurt, it's so damn syrupy, I stand up at the front of the room, scanning the faces. Mr. Collins stands behind me protectively and surveys the room, as well.

Marcel walks up. He has rather shaggy, dark hair and brown eyes. He's a few inches taller than I am and wears a light brown, slightly wrinkled linen blazer over a white, button-down shirt, jeans, and brown leather loafers that look a bit like slippers. He seems as nervous as I am, now that I'm standing in front of my father.

"Roman," he says warmly. He steps closer and envelops me in his arms.

We stay that way for what seems like five minutes. He starts to cry and pulls away, taking a tissue from his front jacket pocket.

"I knew I was going to do that. I've been thinking about this moment since your mom contacted me," he says. "Hey, are you okay? That was a tough opening up there."

"Yeah, not my finest," I answer quietly.

My first feeling after being hugged by Marcel is total, complete relief.

Marcel is the real deal. And I'm his son.

I try not to smile ear to ear like a fool.

"Well, you recovered great. You did great up there. Really." I see the kindness and warmth in his eyes, his wanting me to know not to sweat it.

I know I didn't do great "up there" at first, but I hope people didn't notice. He is one of the few people in the room who understands why I lost my way. Why I was thinking too much. Why I couldn't start my piece.

Mr. Collins come up and shakes hands with Marcel then says to me like he means it, "Well done, Roman. I'm impressed. So, you have permission from your mom to go out with Marcel for dinner, but only if I come with. I'm sure you can understand. But we need to be back at the hotel in two hours." He then explains to Marcel, "We have to get up at 5 a.m. to get to the airport for our flight."

"Sure. Of course," Marcel says.

Dinner is everything I ever imagined it could be. Mr. Collins sits at a nearby table and stays busy with his phone and green folder full of papers.

"I can understand if you want to call me Marcel. But I'll feel honored whenever you are ready to call me Dad," he says.

I want to tell Marcel everything I can think of about me. He tells me he works as the musical director at the Arena of Nîmes, about thirty minutes from his home in Arles. It was built in 70 A.D., so it's freaky old. They have a music festival there every July, so he's super-busy with that right now. He shows me photos of it on his phone, and it honestly looks like a falling-down ancient ruin, not a place where you can have a concert. He says it's been remodeled, and they still have bullfights in it, too, like they did ages ago. When I visit, he says I'll get the complete private tour, so that's really cool.

He then tells me he's been married to his wife, Simone, for almost ten years and has two daughters—Arabella, who is eight, and Fay, who is five.

"So I have sisters?" I ask.

"Yes. And they can't wait to meet you. We haven't shared with them the full story yet, of course, because of their ages. But it will come with time. They drew you these pictures."

He pulls some papers from a pocket inside his blazer and unfolds them. One is a crayon drawing of a purple cow outside a red barn with a yellow sun in the sky. The name Fay is printed in large, unsteady red print. The other is a color pencil sketch of a boy who I assume is supposed to look like me, since he has brown hair. The name Arabella is written neatly in the right corner.

"Wow. Tell them thanks. I love these," I say, pressing out the few wrinkles.

"I've always wanted to visit Chicago. I'd like to bring them, but I think they're a little young right now. Would it be okay if I visit you in early August? That's when regular life really shuts down and Europeans go on holiday."

"That sounds super chill," I say before realizing I may be trying a bit too hard to be cool. To calm myself down while my heart is racing, I take a breath and try again. "That would be great. Mom and I are moving back to L.A., but I don't think that's going to happen super-soon."

"It sounds like Chicago it is then. I've never been to America. There's a lot I'd like to see in Chicago."

"Me, too. I've only been living there since September, and I've done some of the touristy places, like the Museum of Science and Industry, with my grandpa. That's his thing, science. But I don't know Chicago too well. They have this 'L' that is pretty awesome, though. It's like the Tube we've been taking around London, but it's above ground. It goes all over the city."

"I've seen the 'L' in your movies," he says. "When I come, we can check the city out together on it. Do you like baseball?"

"I've been to a bunch of Dodgers games. I don't know the players much. I play basketball. Do you like basketball?

"Sounds like there are a few things you can teach me. I don't really know American basketball or baseball. I do know, in Chicago, you have the Cubs and the White Sox. And the Bulls."

"Grandpa likes the Cubs. I like the L.A. Lakers and the Dodgers. A baseball game would be fun in the summer. I can check to see when the Dodgers are playing the Cubs." The moment I say that, I realize how awesome that day would be.

"Is Michael Jordan a big deal still? He was huge in Europe, even back, what was it, twenty years ago now."

"Yes, everyone in the world likes Mike," I answer. "He's epic."

"I follow football. That's what you Americans call soccer. My club is PSV. But I'd like to learn about baseball. Maybe I can come to one of your basketball games one day, too."

I flash to an image. My father in the stands, cheering for me, as I take it coast to coast. I don't know if I've ever been happier than I am right this moment.

The two hours pass in a flash. When Mr. Collins motions to me it is time to leave, Marcel and I stand, and he again hugs me tightly. I can see he is fighting back more tears.

We ask Mr. Collins to take a photo and hand him both our phones. We pose for photo after photo until I take a step forward and Mr. Collins hands us back the phones.

"Thanks," I say.

"No problem." I could swear Mr. Collins is trying to hold back tears, too. "We've gotta go though."

"Bye, Marcel," I say, slowly walking away. We head back toward the hotel, me talking nonstop about every bit of the conversation and Marcel's impending visit to Chicago.

Back in my hotel room, T.J. is sleeping in his bed, even though the bedside light is still on right next to him. He never adjusted to the time change and has been yawning for the past five days.

I turn over the last few hours in my mind. The competition feels so far in the past, compared with the magnitude of having dinner with Marcel. I know my mom, grandparents, Zuzu, and Claire are all anxious to hear details. I want to hold onto the feelings I have for a bit longer, turn them around, and dissect them every which way.

I put the drawings from my, well, my half-sisters inside my gray leather notebook and then pull out my phone and stare at the photos Mr. Collins snapped of us tonight. I look at me and Marcel side by side and realize we share the same nose, for sure. That he's a little bit taller than me, which is good. I may not become a dangerous three-point shooter, but I see I have the potential to gain some more height advantage at the net.

I climb into bed and try to sleep. After what seems like an hour of staring at the ceiling, I am still amped up. I realize sleep will not come easily. Feeling fully awake, I want to let these emotions out, so I can try to get some shut-eye.

I attach a photo of me and Marcel and group text it to Zuzu and Claire.

So this happened. Tell u more when see u.

I send the photo to Mom, too, writing:

Fill u in when I get back.

CHAPTER SIXTY-SIX

Despite once again scoring the dreaded middle seat on our flight home, after the breakfast service, I maneuver myself around in the tight space and fall asleep. Before I know it, a flight attendant touches my shoulder. I hit the button that pops my seat slightly forward and peer over T.J.'s shoulder as the Chicago skyline and Lake Michigan fill the narrow airplane window view.

As I walk with my group out of Customs, I look around for my mom. It takes me a minute to find her amidst the throng of many moms and dads and siblings.

After giving me a long, tight hug hello, she walks over to Mr. Collins, and they move away from us to talk quietly. I know they are talking about Marcel and Mr. Collins is giving her the whole scoop about our dinner. I watch as the conversation lobs back and forth. Shivani and her mom walk up and, after waiting patiently on the fringe for a minute or two, her mom steps in and interrupts Mr. Collins mid-sentence. Mom quickly nods goodbye and heads back to me.

"Ready?" she asks.

"Yeah, sure. Let me just say goodbye."

I head over to Desmond and T.J., as Desmond playfully reaches out with a fist bump. I play along, and then we both fist bump T.J., me first and then Desmond jokingly. The parents around us smile. Jasmine is with her brother and waves a goodbye in my direction. I wave back and then give a little wave to Emma. Kamara is kneeling down, showing pictures from her phone to a cute kid in braids wearing a purple dress, whom I assume is her younger sister. Annie is talking with her Dad, but Claire is not there as part of her welcome party.

I grab the handle of my wheeled luggage and follow Mom outside to the parking lot. After too many hours waiting in an airport and then sitting cooped up inside an airplane, it feels so good to take in the warm, summer air. We wander onto the surface parking lot. After passing a number of aisles, she walks up to a silver Hyundai Santa Fe and lifts open the rear trunk door.

"Mom, I'm confused. Where's the BMW?"

"I sold it over the weekend. This car makes more sense for us. I found it on Craigslist, if you can believe that. Grandpa helped me sell the BMW. And now I have some walking-around money."

I settle into the front passenger seat and study the sleek black dashboard, homing in on the radio. After I press a few buttons and locate the Bluetooth, the car passes my inspection. I then spend fifteen minutes talking nonstop about the touristy things we did, about the Barbican Young Poets we met, and about Marcel and his daughters. I tell her he is planning a visit this summer, and that we are friends now on Facebook, Twitter, and Instagram.

I come up for air.

"Mom. Airplane food is the worst. Can I get dinner?"

"Well, it's 6:00 p.m., which I believe is midnight in England. Aren't you tired?"

"Kinda. I'm more hungry than tired, though."

We drive to Chipotle, and, after I get my burrito and settle in at a table across from her, Mom lets out a sigh. I've done this enough with her, so I know a newsflash is coming.

"Roman. What if we stayed in Chicago?" she asks quickly.

"Really?" I'm totally confused. I thought L.A. was always her plan.

"Would you like that? I was offered a part-time job at the Chanel makeup counter at Neiman Marcus on Michigan Avenue. I have a few days until I have to give them my answer."

"But what about your classes?"

"Oh, I can finish my training up here. There's beauty schools in Chicago, you know!" She grabs my hand in hers across the table before she continues. "I realize Marcel is going to be part of the picture going forward. I have to admit, I didn't want to go down this road. But now that you've done it—well, we've done it—I actually feel so relieved."

"It would have been a lot easier fifteen years ago!" I say, pointing out what is now obvious to us both.

She grudgingly nods her head then squeezes my hand before letting it go. She gets all serious with me again. "You only have three more years of high school, and I think this is where you should see that through."

"And Eric?" I ask. "Is he part of the reason you're okay staying here?"

"Oh, not at all. It's too early to say that. But I have to be honest, I do like him. He's in the Oak Park Runners' Club and is helping me train for a 5K. Grandpa is thrilled."

"I'll bet!" I laugh. I try, but my mind can't conjure up an image of my mom wearing some generic race T-shirt and standing at the starting line of a 5K.

"It's not easy being the grownup," she says, bringing me back into the moment. "But I feel like I've done the hard work now. I am so proud of you every day. Now I want you to be proud of me."

"Mom, I am. You don't have to worry about that. I'm where I am now because of your fuck-ups." I flash her a playful grin.

She smiles, knowing I speak the truth.

"And I do want to stay at this high school. A lot!"

"Good. It's settled. Let's start looking for an apartment next week. I know this town like the back of my hand. It shouldn't be hard to find something we like. Maybe even something near the high school."

"Wow, Mom, so this is for real?"

"Well, to be honest, L.A. will always be in my blood," she says. "Your grandma helped me really think this through. She's right about the fact that your high school days will be over before we know it. I can tough out a few more of these winters, if you can."

"Barely, Mom. They suck. But the thought of moving again sucks more."

"You've had a lot of big changes this year. I get that."

"One thing I can't *wait* to change is having my own room without a Buddha statute staring at me. Oh, and I'm keeping the PlayStation and TV in my bedroom, right?"

"I don't know. I think that TV is pretty big for a bedroom..."

"Seriously? You're taking my TV away from me now?"

"Don't strong-arm me, buddy. Let's go with I'll think about it."

"Mom. It's my TV, remember?" I realize I'm going to have to do some convincing.

Just then my phone blips.

Claire has sent me a text.

"Hey, Mom, can we take this to go? I have to catch some people up."

"Sure." She snatches up her big, brown, logoed handbag and stands. "Let's go."

I practically float out of the restaurant, holding my wrapped burrito, adrenaline pumping through me as I process all that's become settled in the few hours since I landed at O'Hare Airport.

During the car ride back to my grandparents', I unlock my phone and read Claire's text:

Welcome back. Annie says the trip was awesome.

Yes. Epic. I'll fill you in after I eat. Starving.

You're always starving!

Then I text Zuzu.

Operation Marcel. Case closed.

Is everything good?

I don't hesitate:

Yes. It's all good.

I hit send.

AUTHOR'S NOTE

English teacher Peter Kahn started using Spoken Word in his classroom at Oak Park and River Forest High School (in Oak Park, Illinois) in 1998 and began the school's Spoken Word Club in 1999. He has been at the forefront of the movement to bring Spoken Word into the classroom and help expand the discipline. From 2001–2003, he brought his experiences to London, where he co-founded the London Teenage Poetry Slam. In 2001, he was part of the collective of teachers and writers who helped conceive Louder Than a Bomb, an annual youth poetry competition in Chicago.

However, this is a work of fiction. Teacher Patrick Collins is not Peter Kahn. But without Peter Kahn, there would be no Patrick Collins. Thank you, Peter, for welcoming me into the world of spoken word and explaining how the magic happens. As Peter will tell you, poems have to be strong on the page before they can get to the stage.

It has been an honor to witness the teenagers in Spoken Word Club at Oak Park and River Forest High School, with their different interests and backgrounds, stand up on stage and colorfully share their struggles and successes in a room that overflows with support and respect. They give me hope for the future.

Melanie Weiss

ABOUT THE AUTHOR

Melanie Weiss lives and works in Oak Park, Illinois. This is her first novel, but it won't be her last.

www.melanie-weiss.com

Made in the USA
Middletown, DE
17 March 2019